IT WAS A FREEWILL RAPTURE

Day of the Lord DIARIES
~ Book One ~

DAVID ALAN SMITH

outskirts press

It Was A Freewill Rapture
Day of the Lord Diaries Book One
All Rights Reserved.
Copyright © 2022 David Alan Smith
v5.0

This is a work of fiction. Names, characters, businesses, places, events, locales, and incidents are either the products of the author's imagination or used in a fictitious manner. Any resemblance to actual persons, living or dead, or actual events is purely coincidental.

The opinions expressed in this manuscript are solely the opinions of the author and do not represent the opinions or thoughts of the publisher. The author has represented and warranted full ownership and/or legal right to publish all the materials in this book.

This book may not be reproduced, transmitted, or stored in whole or in part by any means, including graphic, electronic, or mechanical without the express written consent of the publisher except in the case of brief quotations embodied in critical articles and reviews.

Outskirts Press, Inc.
http://www.outskirtspress.com

ISBN: 978-1-9772-4732-2

Cover Photo © 2022 www.gettyimages.com. All rights reserved - used with permission.

Outskirts Press and the "OP" logo are trademarks belonging to Outskirts Press, Inc.

PRINTED IN THE UNITED STATES OF AMERICA

PART ONE
'...THE FALLING AWAY...'

2 Thessalonians 2:1-3 *Now, brethren, concerning the coming of our Lord Jesus Christ and our gathering together to Him. Let no one deceive you by any means; for that Day will not come unless the falling away comes first.*

-Chapter One-
TRUTH NEUTRALITY

2043..., it is yet another year that many Christians await what they've long called 'the Rapture'. As foretold in the Bible, in so many words, it'll be a day that will change the world in unimaginable ways. The world however was already forever changed despite the Rapture's debut.

It was a new world; a world that had succumbed to the sociopolitical ideologies of the Left. America was the last of civilizations to be devoured by what some called 'the beast'. It didn't take long once its teeth were sharpened.

Empowered by the Democrat Party, a new group of anti-American Leftist called Woke Liberals took their grievances to new heights. They waged a fierce, hard-hitting cultural war against the Traditional Conservatives; similar to embittered teenage malcontents waging war against their parents. The war, however, wasn't called the 'Vindictive Teenage Ingrates Kill the Parents to take over the Estate War', or the mirror image of Satan's Rebellion in Heaven; even though that's how some would see it. No..., it was instead called the 'Cancel-Culture Movement'.

It was a pseudo-Marxist crusade where equality was more about 'getting even'; like revenge. Fairness was more about saying, "It's our turn to be superior and privileged." It was a new brand of Civil Rights. They called it 'Equity'.

Thus, America's time-tested stronghold touting 'United We Stand' crumbled into a coalition of liberal tribes in the Democrat Party on one hand; each demanding their fair share of supremacy, power, and identity recognition. On the other hand — the Rightwing Conservatives; now condemned and dubbed the damnable enemy.

As the tribes grew more and more powerful, proving to be unstoppable; the Conservatives eventually found themselves being nothing more than a form of chemotherapy slowing the cancer of Liberalism down. As for the Liberals? They saw themselves more like a cure; a political elixir or crusaders righting the wrongs and saving the world from the oppressive, and stupid, small-minded Conservatives stricken with the age-old disease of traditional parental control, guidance,

IT WAS A FREEWILL RAPTURE

virtues, and discipline that stemmed from America's Judeo-Christian founding. Both staked their claim as having just cause. Both deemed themselves patriotic.

After a long, grueling campaign demonizing America's historical upbringing and every aspect of Conservatism by using the most sinister and devious of tactics; Liberalism inevitably prevailed. Its presence and influence were so dominant that it managed to seat itself at the core of all religions. In turn, despite a political ideology — Liberalism was rapidly becoming the makings of a 'one world religion'; if it hadn't already.

A self-exalting fabrication of love coupled with an obsession of exaggerated concern is its optics and theme; so beautiful and godly, but Totalitarian Conformity is its rule; making it dark, hostile, and ugly — Nazis-like in nature. Instead of a society threatening…, "you're either a Nazis — or else", it was a society threatening, "you're either Woke — or else."

Noncompliance quickly became disobedience and did not, and would not go unnoticed. The watchful eyes and unholy alliance between the myriads of Liberal tattletales and the Deep State would see to that; especially since 'One Nation Under God' had changed into 'One Nation Under Surveillance'. Over time, a short but telling mantra emerged from the Woke Liberals tyrannical iron fist; 'There's a price to pay if you don't

DAVID ALAN SMITH

obey.' Both the Right and the Left knew it by heart; but they'd recite it from opposite perspectives.

The Left sang it loud and strong as an intimidating threat. The Right, however, whispered it quietly amongst themselves as a strong advisory; like warning children to stay on the beaten path—or else. They had to be extra careful of many things; to which they were ordered to obey and pay homage to. If not, they'd face an endless onslaught of scorn and retaliation armed with mob-mentality. They'd be ridiculed and shamed to no end; often violent.

Manmade Climate-Change Prevention, Science, Social Justice, Critical Race Theory, Systemic Racism, Marxism, Grade School Sexual-Orientation Education, Trans-Gender Identification, Open Borders, Gun Control, Censorship, Socialized Medicine, Vaccine Passports, Mask Mandates; just to name a few. They became nothing short of idols—'golden calves' by which to worship; on a mandatory basis no less. They were no longer humanitarian suggestions, or sanctimonious products on the Liberals 'wish list'; they were now fanatically enforced laws and morals of the land.

In America, now called the United STATE of America, in order to completely galvanize the Cancel-Culture Movement and solidify Woke-Liberal Supremacy, Christianity needed to be altered, not removed, not even subjugated—just reformed and

IT WAS A FREEWILL RAPTURE

neutralized. Consequently, 'Truth Neutrality' also became the law of the land.

Riding on the holier-than-thou heels of 'Political Correctness', which was already the law of the land, 'Truth Neutrality' was concocted to destroy America's last bastion of Conservatism. It was implemented to purge the last remaining remnant of far Rightwing Christian extremists out of society to purify society; leaving Liberals in complete control over all facets of Christendom. 'No Conservative Christians allowed'; as Woke-Christianity would have it.

The scheme by which to weed out the extremists boiled down to yet another nationwide mandate. Targeting and isolating all professing Christians; the STATE imposed a two-part inquiry. It was just two very simple questions, but they were extremely indicative; enough to separate the goats from the sheep.

The first. 'Is Jesus…a way…to heaven…, or is Jesus…the way…to heaven?' That question alone was enough to separate most Christians. For those who answered 'Jesus is…the way…to heaven'; a follow up question would be processed. 'Is this…the truth…, or is it merely…a belief…?' Like the Spanish Inquisition, wrong answers in what many called the 'Woke Inquisition' cost dearly.

The incriminating questions were cleverly designed to force all Christians, the Christian religions,

DAVID ALAN SMITH

Christian churches, Christian schools, Christian organizations, corporations and businesses to inadvertently, and officially, denounce Jesus Christ by demoting and cheapening his claims, his ministry, miracles and resurrection to that of bedtime stories and legends harmless enough to believe, but deemed untrue; like pots of gold at the ends of rainbows, leprechauns, unicorns, and Santa Claus.

Ultimately, comic books and Saturday morning tales from purple dinosaurs and yellow sponges was to have more credence. With that, giving the impression of upholding America's 'freedom of religion' and dubbing themselves magnanimous; the STATE allowed Christians to practice their faith and worship as they please as long as they openly and publicly confessed what they believed wasn't the truth, but limited to a... 'belief only'...status. In turn, grant them citizenship; exempt from persecution, prosecution, and penalization.

Most Christians; Christians of all sorts, and all the Christian religions, already watered down and liberalized to one degree or another; immediately welcomed 'Truth Neutrality' with open arms. They had no qualms whatsoever giving the STATE the answers they wanted to hear. Believing it to be in the name of love and another universal ingredient to add to their *forms of godliness*'; they happily embraced the new

IT WAS A FREEWILL RAPTURE

law. When it was all said and done; they were eager to sign and publicly post the official affidavit to certify their conformity to the quasi 'one world religion' dogma…; 'Liberal First—Faith and Religion Second'.

Others were a little more reluctant; but for the most part easily swayed to comply with the new law for many different reasons. In most cases, whether they agreed or not; giving the STATE the answers they wanted to hear and signing the 'comply and conform' affidavit was a small price to pay to be left alone. Still, there were others—the extremists, who just couldn't bring themselves to follow suit.

To them, for Jesus to say…, '…*deny me amongst men, and I will deny you to the Father*' had a little more of an impact than just a small handful of words jotted down in the thick of the Bible. Even though interpreted in many ways, the lone scripture was still edgy enough to convince some to play on the side of caution; to think it wise not to second guess it.

It could be said they feared the STATE, but their fear of GOD was far greater. The fear of losing their 'salvation' dwarfed any and all fear they had of the STATE. Losing their souls for the sake of securing a seat in the Politically Correct Coliseum, only to watch their unwavering brothers and sisters in Christ being eaten alive by the Woke-Liberal Lions just wasn't something they wanted to conform to—let alone live with.

DAVID ALAN SMITH

Consequently, the Conservative Christian extremists floated to the top of the barrel of mainstream Christianity like water in oil; making it particularly easy for the STATE to pluck 'the goats' out of society so as to sanitize and secure their Marxist Utopia of Democrat Tribes and Liberal Do-Gooders.

Conservative Catholics, Mormons, Evangelicals, or Christians in general; if they did not conform to the Woke Liberals new and improved Christian faith touting 'Truth Neutrality'…; faith that does not offend — they were immediately declared to be haters, dividers, and insurrectionists; even 'Enemies of the State' and 'Domestic Terrorists'. They were lumped together and officially renamed 'Jesus Fundamentalists', called Jef's for short. It was the official name, but in the streets, in the schools, the Media and Hollywood; to be called a Jef was derogatory and spiteful. It referred to 'Jesus Freaks'.

Now marked and segregated; public outcasts, stains in their former religions, churches, and congregations, feeling unwelcome and no longer comfortable in gatherings full of gossip and glares, having nowhere else to turn but to themselves, the Jesus Fundamentalists, amongst themselves, called themselves and each other 'Born Agains'. It was endearing and affectionate, but more importantly; it seemed fitting.

By Biblical terms; only those… *'born of the spirit'* …, whose faith and trust in the Gospel of Jesus Christ and

IT WAS A FREEWILL RAPTURE

the Word of God is like that of a wide-eyed little child totally believing their parents without even the slightest hint of doubt would be so willing to do what they have chosen to do. 'Born of the spirit'…, or crazy—it was one or the other. And there were plenty of cult-like Christian lunatics who too refused to comply with 'Truth Neutrality'. For them, *'born of the spirit'* has always been questionable—but then again…, who isn't…?

GOD…, of course, knows the difference; according to the Bible. Jesus on High and His angels know the difference…; as does Satan—the devil. He too, as well as his immeasurable army of malevolent demons who loath the human-kind with a burning passion; they all know who is or isn't *'born again'*.

Either way, the price Jesus Fundamentalists would pay for their defiance, or devotion to Christ depending how one would define it, was severe. Failure to comply with 'Truth Neutrality' after a handful of opportunities and chances would consist of being sent to Sensitivity Camps for rehabilitation, but not without first losing everything of value. Their jobs, careers, their homes, businesses and property, even their children were callously seized by the STATE.

Why…? Why go to such extremes…? It mystified the Right as to why. As for the Left? They had plenty of reasons why; and countless excuses. One could ask them why they teach their young to instinctively step on the Jesus Fundamentalists, Conservatives, and Zionists like cockroaches scurrying across the floor; and you'd get the same answers as to why they've gone to such extremes.

They had a whole litany of explanations to combat the Right and eliminate any influence they had on humanity and civilization. There were some though, who dared to say there was really only one reason for the Liberals sanitation crusade, and that would be their utter hatred for the Right; pure resentment.

Often compared to the hatred in the hearts of racists and anti-Semites; the Left's hatred for the Right seemed unnatural — demonic, they believed. Whether it is or isn't, the fact remained; the Liberals, more particularly the Woke Liberals, thrived to despise the Right, often with a teeth-gnashing kind of antipathy. So much so that most of them had no scruples whatsoever forming an alliance with the likes of Communist China, the Soviets, and the Muslim Brotherhood to help rip and tear Conservatism out of the fabric of America with a vengeance.

Of course…, the liberal's hatred has always been justified because it's deemed to be in the name of love; as taught to their offspring. It's an odd kind of love though. It's as if they'd measure their love and godliness by how much they'd hate the Right. The more they'd jeer, criticize and condemn the more righteous

IT WAS A FREEWILL RAPTURE

they'd deem themselves to be.

One could only wish they had learned how ugly it was of certain groups in the past measuring their sense of righteousness by how much they'd hate those not like them. It was in fact these very groups of people the Liberals claimed to be fighting and denouncing. Sadly, the only thing they learned from all the 'righteous haters' in the past was to replicate them with their own version of 'righteous hatred'. Like all the others, their pursuit of perfecting humanity by the process of elimination and world dominance was just as intoxicating; as it was ugly.

Still…, it's love. Who can argue with love? Who could argue with hatred in the name of love? Love is beautiful. Love is godly.

On this particular day, two brothers on a little road trip were once again faced with the challenge; trying to figure out how so many people so full of love find their hatred to be so beautiful and godly. For Randy and Joel; the mystery would only deepen. Not only that; the beautiful and godly hatred they find so strange and so hard to understand was about to get even uglier.

1Thessolonians 1-3 *But concerning the times and the seasons, brethren, you have no need that I should write to you. For you yourselves know perfectly that the day of the Lord so comes as a thief in the night. For when they say, "Peace and Security!" then sudden destruction comes upon them, as labor pains upon a pregnant woman. And they shall not escape.*

-Chapter Two-
QUASI GESTAPO

"What time is it?" Joel nervously asked.

"Uh, let's see — time for you to tell me again how great and how awesome of a brother I am." Randy joked.

"Oh, yeah right!" Joel bounced back with a chuckle.

Randy looked at his watch. "It's ten after six. We've got plenty of time."

As they inched their way to the check point, Joel shifted and repositioned himself in Randy's ol' pride-and-joy; his blue '64 Chevy pickup. "You know, I love this old truck, but you gotta do something about these seats, dude. I feel like I'm sitting on a concrete bench."

"Stop complaining! We look cool." Randy playfully insisted.

IT WAS A FREEWILL RAPTURE

"Oh yeah, we look really cool, Randy. Give me a break—maybe twenty-five years ago, but being that were both headed for fifty in a couple years I'd hardly say we look cool. Unless of course you mean in a dinosaur sort of way—there're lots of people who think they're cool."

Randy had to laugh. Frustrated though, he went on to remark, "Man, I just hate these things."

"Yeah, I know. Me, too," Joel dreadfully agreed, "me too."

One by one, car by car they'd get closer and closer to the random scan by DSS (Domestic Security and Surveillance). It was slow, but they at least had a beautiful view. Coming out of South Lake Tahoe, Hwy 50, headed for Reno, they were atop the lower mountainside looking down on Carson City peacefully sitting at the bottom of the valley.

Early in the morning, it was sunrise. The sun was just peeking over the top of the mountain with all its glory. Rays of light seemingly piercing holes and glimmering through sporadic portals in the rain clouds made it especially striking. Carson City stood out like a gem. Long past its heyday, seeing the old nostalgic little town briefly lit up sort of revived it, at least from a distance.

It was a beautiful sight, but it was also sad. Carson City was one of many cities dying in the wake of

DAVID ALAN SMITH

modern America's so-called progress and saving the planet. It was sad for those like Joel and Randy who saw it for what it was, but for most, it was just normal.

Finally, after about twenty minutes of waiting, Randy turned down the radio as they slowly made their way towards eight stone-faced militants in raingear and head-cams. The 'King's Men', is what many had sarcastically come to call them. They were the product of America's fundamental transformation; the policing branch of DSS. What was once called the police, or cops, are now called Enforcers; short for Social Enforcers.

Faction Eight Global Police is their official name; Faction Eight referring to America as the eighth faction of ten across the globe. Men in blue they were not; they were of a vivid green. It was a far cry from military green or the green of ICE, now abolished. It was closer to an environmental green; a clean sort of green symbolizing peace and closeness to nature. Even though it came across as a sort of happy color in the eyes of children; they were most intimidating.

At the height of America's Cancel-Culture Movement, instead of eradicating the police of whom were demonized and forever accused of racism by the Left; it was politically decided to alter and restructure 'Law Enforcement'. Policing was now all about enforcing 'social crimes'; things that offended people,

16

IT WAS A FREEWILL RAPTURE

things that didn't do enough or even say enough to propagate Civil Equity, as well as things that violated the environment, the climate, and the planet.

Like most of the enforcers, the roadside regiment there to greet Randy and Joel were young; mid-thirties max — six men and two women, in this case. Their youth however didn't change the fact that they were grim. Being that it was a bit gusty and facing them under a blanket of swirling, dark and heavy clouds only made them look that much worse. They came across as menacing and unfriendly.

Regardless, the enforcers were there to 'protect and to serve'. As always and by law, they took the oath. Of course, the times had changed. Their priorities and orders had change. They were there to 'protect and serve' alright, but it was the A-Class Elitists, the B-Class State, and the Planet they'd be protecting and serving. Being a part of the State, to be an enforcer was very convenient. Taking an oath to 'protect and serve' themselves as B-Class Citizens only embolden them to push their authority to the limit; and then some.

It was the typical double talk so commonly used by the Leftwing demagogues; seasoned Liberals, Progressives, Marxists, Socialist, Communist, Democrats, and turncoat Republicans — fill in the blank..., they were all the same. Teaching children and getting the commoners to understand rule number one; which is to say protecting and serving those who are in charge of protecting the Planet, protecting the Environment, protecting the Social Balance, and protecting Humanity is, in a roundabout way, protecting and serving the People. It was all about sustainability and security.

How good of them. So much love…, so thoughtful and godly; how could anyone think otherwise? Right now, Randy and Joel were on the verge of getting another dose of some of that love and concern there to protect them and serve them for their own good.

"It ticks me off to know our taxes are actually paying these asshole thugs to harass us." Randy quietly grumbled to Joel as they slowly came to a stop. Taking his voice down another notch while rolling down his window he turned to Joel and whispered one more little grievance before having to face the music.

"It just sucks, to know they slap a frickin' toll on us too every time we're forced to go through these stupid things."

Even though it was softly spoken, Joel heard it loud and clear. Needless to say, he had the same sentiments. It didn't take a rocket scientist to figure out these mandated checkpoints wasn't so much about security as it was collecting funds to feed the State and its insatiable appetite for lucrative living. It was irritating, even infuriating if one so chose to gnaw on it long enough.

IT WAS A FREEWILL RAPTURE

The eight enforcers promptly took formation around the truck, following protocol to the tee. Two circled the perimeter; one from a distance with a Visual Probe — scanning for weapons, ammunition or contraband hidden in the truck and the other with a trained dog sniffing out what the Visual Probe might have missed.

They were all armed with assault rifles, but by far, the most powerful weapon in their arsenal was in the hands of the CDO (Check and Document Officer). He's the one that posed the biggest threat because he's the one armed with an AP18; a lightweight portable CPU (central processing unit) and database. It gave the Faction Eight Global Police everything they needed to know when it came to pointing their guns to the ground or targeting in on people. They called the powerful little unit MOM, an acronym — Monocular Observation Module.

Having been through it before, both Randy and Joel already had their ID's out. They knew the routine. Being herded and funneled into a checkpoint like cattle was only part of the time-consuming humiliation. They'd also have to jump through the hoops of questions and balance the pains of interrogation on the tips of their noses to appease the quasi-Gestapo.

Now stopped and the engine turned off, Randy and Joel sat quietly; waiting for the enforcers to 'protect

DAVID ALAN SMITH

and serve' them. With a cautious approach—giving the inside of the cab and truck bed a quick once over, the CDO flaunting his AP18 proceeded to Randy's open window.

"Good morning, gentlemen," rolled out of the officer's mouth. "Are you chipped?" he asked.

"No sir, we are not." Randy replied as he did his best to ignore the head-cam recording his every move and word. Even though both he and Joel have been through it before, being video recorded still made it very awkward and uncomfortable to say the least.

"ID's and Domestic Passports please." the officer requested. Randy handed them over to be scanned. Within seconds, all was well on the CDO's monitor and earpiece. The ID's and Passports matched the Facial Recognition Scan. Also, no red alerts—just some standard yellow and orange flags.

"Are there any firearms or ammunition with you, on you or in the vehicle?" he asked with authority.

"No Sir!" Randy promptly answered.

The officer paused momentarily. He took a gander at his monitor, looked up and dialed in on Randy.

"Randall Alan Stevenson," he said almost in a tone of interrogating a prisoner. "I see here that you have a Smith and Wesson .38 Special Revolver. Do you still have this weapon?"

20

IT WAS A FREEWILL RAPTURE

"Yes..., yes I do."

Glancing back down to his screen, "How about this uhh — this Remington 12-gauge shotgun? Do you still have this weapon?"

"Yes, I do."

"Are there or have there been any more weapons added to your civilian arsenal?"

"No sir!"

"Very good — because you do know that you can only have two firearms in your possession. Is this not correct Mr Stevenson?" the officer asked with his eyes fixated on the monitor.

"Yes sir — only two. I am aware."

"Is your arsenal still located at 2625 Pine Valley, South Lake Tahoe, California?"

"Yes!"

"Are they locked, unloaded, Child Proof, and up to the Safety Standards and Codes?"

"Yes, yes they are."

The officer pondered. "Hmmm..., I see here that you were OK'd on a random home search and compliance inspection last year. Good. I see you've complied with the Semi-Automatic Weapon Relinquishment Laws. Good. How 'bout uhh — let's see here — State issued ammo? Are you still in compliance as to having in your possession twelve rounds or less for these two weapons?" he asked.

∽ 21 ∽

DAVID ALAN SMITH

Randy couldn't help but feel like a common criminal having to answer to a Parole Officer. He also couldn't help but feel a bit of resentment. He did well to bite his tongue though. Hiding his anger, he went on to answer once again, respectfully and to the point. "Yes…, yes on both of those questions."

"Six .38 caliber bullets and…, says here—six shotgun shells purchased …, gosh—over a year ago on Ammo.Gov. Still have 'em, huh? Haven't gotten anymore…., on the black market?" He probed.

"No sir. That's all I have. At ten bucks a pop…, you know—per cartridge…, can't afford to just use 'em up. Never know when you'll need 'em for protection." Randy added to patronize the officer; telling him what he figured he wanted to hear.

"Yep…! That's why we still uphold the Second Amendment." The officer praised like it was a wonderful thing letting people have a gun or two with no more than twelve bullets. It irked Randy. He sneered inside; mentally gnashing his teeth in anger, yet he didn't show it.

"Second Amendment…, my ass," he thought to himself, Joel too for that matter. The officer was quick to brag about Randy's right to own a gun, but nothing about paying with his life if he'd dare break the iron-fisted guidelines and restrictions that came with it. The 'Second Amendment' was now nothing

IT WAS A FREEWILL RAPTURE

short of a joke. What became of it is a travesty, just like the First Amendment.

After documenting the answer, the officer unexpectedly took a casual step back so as to admire Randy's old truck. "Wow! You sure don't see very many of these ol' guys anymore. What is it — a sixty-four? Sixty-five?" the officer politely asked.

"It's a sixty-four. I've had it for a while, thirty years at least." Randy boasted.

"Yep...!" the officer noted. "It's kind of a shame that this time next year these old vehicles will no longer be street legal outside of parades, exhibitions and Hollywood contracts. But, as you know, it's for the best. It's really too bad that they do so much damage to the environment and disrupt the climate. My granddad used to have one." he added. "Oh well — what's the odometer reading?"

Randy looked down through the steering wheel and cited the numbers clearly rolled over two, maybe even three times. "Uhh, let's see..., 2-2-3-1-1-2."

The officer peered into the window to verify Randy's answer and skimmed over his AP18 monitor. "Well, you're good there too. Out of the 500 miles allotted to you this year, you still have another 293 miles left. Good for you — no citation. Better use them miles up though before the ban, huh."

Randy could only nod, but he managed to do it

∽ 23 ∽

without rolling his eyes in disgust. He kept his cool, went along to get along. The whole time though, it was Joel that he was more worried about. He's the one that's going to be put to the test; who's really going to face the music — head on.

John 15:18-19 *"If the world hates you, you know that it hated Me before it hated you. If you were of the world, the world would love its own. Yet because you are not of the world, but I chose you out of the world, therefore the world hates you."*

Jesus

-Chapter Three-
JESUS FREAK

Finished with Randy, the officer promptly shifted his attention to Joel silently sitting on the passenger side. Joel was outwardly calm, but inside he was leery and anxious. The officer modestly glanced into the cab past Randy and got a good look at him. He went directly to his touch screen and MOM told him everything there was to know about Joel.

From there the officer knew enough to know he didn't care for him at all. Unlike Randy having to answer to a yellow flag alert stipulating firearms, Joel had to answer to an orange flag — an affiliation alert. It was the kind of alert that turned a standard interrogation into a rude and contentious hate fest.

Grimacing, the smug enforcer looked in at his

DAVID ALAN SMITH

subject quietly waiting to be questioned. He just stared at Joel as he listened to Communal Intel brief him through his earpiece. It was awkward. The guy just standing there staring at him; it made him feel really uncomfortable. It was however only a handful of seconds. Still, even that was too long as far as Joel was concerned.

Once again, likened to an interrogation the officer would follow up:

"So! Who do we have here? Jonathon Joel Stevenson. Stevenson…, Stevenson? Randall Stevenson and Jonathon Stevenson; so—you boys married?" he obnoxiously asked with a smirk and loud enough to get a rise out of his comrades in arms.

"Funny!" Randy said with a half-hearted go-along laugh. "No, we're brothers," he added so as to answer the question respectfully.

"Yeah—I can see the resemblance, but I wasn't talking to you was I?" the officer rudely asserted. He again fixated on Joel and continued his snide inquiry.

"Well now, Jonathon. I see here that you've been flagged with a big, bright orange icon here on the database. How 'bout that? Well, let's see here—you're not a Catholic, you're not a Mormon—says here that you're uh, a Jef—a Jesus-Freak. OOP's!" he quickly blurted. "Oh…! I'm so sorry Mr. Stevenson. I meant to say Jesus Fundamentalist. Please forgive me. You

IT WAS A FREEWILL RAPTURE

know—sometimes I just get this big giant official JF reference on my monitor a little mixed up with the street lingo. You know how it is?" he sarcastically explained knowing darn well it wasn't a mistake.

His phony apology and tone resonated loud and clear. Both Joel and Randy knew right away where he stood and what he thought about Christians. The hatred, resentment, the ridicule and mocking; Joel's gone through it many times over. What's one more? Still, he was tense. Already knowing where the officer was going, he braced himself and waited for the onslaught of questions he'd have to answer as well as everything else in between.

"So! Is it true, Mr Stevenson? Is MOM here telling the truth? Are you a Jef—one of them Born Agains?" the officer briskly asked with a sneer.

"Yes sir. Yes I am." Joel nervously answered.

"You know it's laughable to think just how many there are of you who still have the word 'sin' in your vocabulary. Humph! It doesn't matter, I guess. You still have to obey the law.

You know Mr Stevenson..., the Catholics, Mormons, Muslims and Jews, most of them have enough sense to comply and conform to the Truth Neutrality Legislation. I mean hell..., even a bunch of your creepy Christian denominations have enough sense. But you Jesus Fundamentalists—you're a...,

27

DAVID ALAN SMITH

well—I don't want to say stupid. I'd say you're a stubborn breed aren't you? And here you are Mr Stevenson. It looks like you're one of 'em. Looks like you're a little reluctant to comply. Looks like you're having a little problem with obeying the law."

Keeping his roadside investigation on point he'd take another look at his monitor. "Let's see here—oh brother," he hissed shaking his head, "another Israel lover? Geez…, whatever! Well, your phone calls and emails look clean—no guns, no Climate Change Denial citations or anything else to suggest you're violent or hostile. But…!" he announced as he looked up again at Joel. "You're still on the list—under investigation. You've been tagged a domestic agitator Mr Stevenson—a threat to our peace and security. That's not good." He stressed and continued.

"As you well know I'm required by law to ask you a couple of simple little questions here so as to confirm exactly where you stand in our society. I'm sure you and your brother here understand? We really do need to know who the troublemakers are—you know—the Uniters and the Dividers. We need to know who's with us and who is against us if we're ever gonna evolve, progress, and synchronize as a society."

Even though the officer spoke nicely, he was most intimidating; especially with an armed unit backing him up. Joel already knew the questions he'd be asked

∽ 28 ∽

IT WAS A FREEWILL RAPTURE

to answer. So did Randy, for that matter. They had already briefly discussed it as soon as they unexpectedly found themselves facing another random checkpoint.

Seconds passed. Joel was ready. So was the officer as he proceeded to ask his questions in the name of the law.

"Well now…, let's see if you've had a change of heart since your last inquisition. So…, which is it, Mr Stevenson? Is Jesus…a way…to heaven? Or is Jesus… the way…to heaven?"

Being the same exact question, he's been getting in the Federal Census for the last five years along with all the other random roadside inquisitions, Joel was well aware of the answer he was supposed to give. But once again he already knew he just couldn't give them that answer. Having a higher obligation, an obligation to God — to Jesus Christ, he simply refused to submit.

"Well…? Which is it?" the officer prodded impatiently.

"The way…," Joel affirmed, "Jesus is the way to heaven."

"Humph," the officer muttered as he jeered at Joel with a hateful smirk. Displeased, he slowly shook his head and went on to finish his Check and Document procedures.

"Well, that's one down and one to go," he said. "All is not lost though, right? You can still redeem

DAVID ALAN SMITH

yourself in spite of your—let us say, hallelujah answer to the first question. You wanna restore your citizenship? You wanna reestablish yourself in society? You wanna be able to vote again? If so, I suggest you comply with the law and give us the answer we need to hear."

Clearly in no mood for nonsense, the officer looked directly at Joel, locked eyes and glared at him. He'd set the stage with a few spiteful remarks though before he'd shoot Joel with the second question.

"You and your kind," he hissed. You sit there and say Jesus is the one and only way to heaven—go around tellin' us if we don't receive Jesus as God and Savior we'll go to hell. Give me a break…! Second question…!" he snapped with malice.

"Is this a belief…, Mr Stevenson? Or is it the truth?" he grilled with the perfect blend of delight and intimidation.

Joel's heart was pounding. In his lap, his hands were trembling. A trickle of sweat streamed down the side of his temple as his gut cramped up in knots, but to his credit, he wasn't about to waver. Or was he…?

For a split moment, to say 'it's just a belief' crept to the tip of his tongue. Temptation was inviting him with a smile and offering him relief. For the sake of being left alone, he stuttered and just about said it. He came within a breath away from giving in. But…, he didn't.

IT WAS A FREEWILL RAPTURE

He snapped out of it and squashed the thought as fast as it crept in. After that, there was no thinking twice about which answer to give. Now, if he could only just spit it out.

His slight hesitation, however, wasn't going over so well. Being tongue-tied and choked up didn't bring him any sympathy from the menacing enforcer breathing down his neck. Extremely impatient and already bitter, he quickly followed up—more firmly, more direct, more hostile.

"Well...? Which is it Mr Born Again Christian? Is it a belief ...? Or is it the truth...?" he sternly pressed.

"It's the truth!" Joel asserted, but nervously.

The answer burned the officer up. Sneering with utter disgust, cross and irritated, he slightly shook his head and hurriedly moved to finish up.

"Ok!" he sharply snapped. "Well that's number seven—number seven out of ten. By law, I'm to tell you that you have three and only three more chances to change your mind, or let us say, change your answer. If you do not comply by or on the tenth inquisition you will be arrested on sight and sent directly to the Camp with the rest of your buddies unwilling to conform to our Coexist Laws and Climate Change Legislation. No trial, and all property confiscated by Global Affairs. Do you understand, Mr Stevenson?" the officer sternly warned.

DAVID ALAN SMITH

"Yes sir! I do." Joel softly replied.

"What was that...? I couldn't hear you—you little Jef...! DO YOU UNDERSTAND...?" he barked, like a drill sergeant shouting down a measly recruit.

"Yes...! Yes I do." Joel again answered, loud enough to make it clear; very clear.

Randy sat there like a rock; quiet and still—holding his breath. He was so disenchanted with everything. He found it hard to comprehend that America had sank to such dismal standards. It was ridiculous, but nevertheless quite the reality. As Randy pondered, the officer would have the last word. He moved to wrap it up because the sprinkling had turned into a slight drizzle.

"Where you guys headed anyhow?" he asked.

"Reno," Randy promptly answered, "to the airport."

The officer stepped back from the door window a bit, just enough to take a proud, cocky stance and look Joel in eye without having to slouch down. Feeling the need to scold Joel; wanting to give him a piece of his mind, he laid into him.

"You know how many people have died and how many frickin' wars have been started because of people like you? Goin' around, looking down your noses; telling the rest of us that you own the truth—you people make me sick. Well, I got news for you—you lil' piss-ant insurrectionist. You don't own the truth.

∽ 32 ∽

IT WAS A FREEWILL RAPTURE

And sooner or later we're gonna get rid of you self-righteous creeps and haters. And just between us..., the sooner the better!"

That was definitely a threat, if there ever was one. At least that's how Joel took it; Randy too, for that matter. The two of them could feel the vitriol in the officer's voice. It was thick and coarse. And the glare in his eye's was full of daggers.

They both knew if the officer could, he'd yank Joel out of the truck right then and there and haul him off to the Camp. If it had been Joel's tenth inquisition, he would have gladly done so. Randy was afraid. He felt like the officer was about to go out of his way to find something..., anything to arrest them or give them a citation.

He so hated to be at their mercy, but there was nothing they could do. So, like Joel, he just waited and hoped it to be over so they could be on their way. They wouldn't be so lucky.

Not quite finished and clearly with an axe to grind, "Hey..., Jesus Freak." The enforcer halfway shouted. "Do yourself a favor...! Renounce your claim on the truth and maybe we'll be nicer to you. And another thing, you might want to rethink your dumb-ass support for those frickin' little troublemakers over in Israel too. Like you, there's nothing good about Zionists."

At that point, the officer quickly glanced up at

DAVID ALAN SMITH

the sky assessing the rainfall getting heavier. He was done. He stepped up to the window, handed Randy their ID's, stepped back and waved them on.

Randy gladly started the truck, put it in gear and like a dog with its tail between its legs, he speedily crept on out of the tense gauntlet of questions and answers. He too was a little shaky. It was nerve racking.

It again made him angry to think he, with his tax dollars, was the one paying these guys to interrogate and badger them and treat them like lower life forms and criminals. There was just something so wrong about it. Paying people to make your life miserable was something that America was never supposed to do, but that's what the Democrats and good-for-nothing Republicans kept voting for; that and enslavement by way of normalizing a dependency on the Government.

After driving a few hundred yards away from their little nightmare, getting away as fast as he could and catching his breath, Randy had to speak up. As if the roadside interrogation wasn't enough, being also a bit agitated at Joel, he took up where the enforcer left off.

"Man, I thought for sure he was going to pull something out of his ass to impound the truck, or give us a citation or even arrest us. Dude! Give it up!" he hammered. "Can you just give it up? Why do you have to keep on insisting your Gospel crap is the truth when

IT WAS A FREEWILL RAPTURE

you know darn well it's just a belief?"

"It's because it isn't just a belief, Randy. It is the truth," Joel gently argued. If it's just a belief then it's like…, I don't know—like goin' around tellin' people I believe what Jesus believed. I mean how stupid is that?"

"Ah jeez…, all I'm sayin' is—you only got three more chances, Joel. They're gonna haul your ass to one these stupid camps—might as well be prison. These people hate you. I mean…, damn—the glare in that enforcer's eyes. I think he wanted to kill you; he probably would have if he knew he'd get away with it."

"Yeah, well…, Jesus said if they hate us to remember it's because they hate him first."

"Wow…, that's comforting." Randy retorted, rolling his eyes. His frustration however didn't stop there.

"Man…, I just don't get it. You can still believe it's the truth, Joel—they don't care. I don't care—nobody cares…! It's like the Christmas thing." Randy reminded, "We can believe it's the birth of Christ all we want. I mean, just because they banned Nativity Scenes and…, and saying 'Merry Christmas' in public doesn't make it not true. Just tell 'em it's a belief and be done with it. They'll leave you alone and you can get on with your life." He pressed.

Joel just looked down and heavily sighed. "You know what—I just can't do that, Randy. I just can't."

∽ 35 ∽

he somberly confessed.

Gathering his thoughts, "These people..., I don't know—it just pisses me off—what they're doing. All this Truth Neutrality crap—how they're forcing us to renounce Jesus; getting us to say he's nothing more than a myth—another manmade belief. It sucks...! It's evil...!" Joel grumbled. "It comes from the depths of hell—from Satan."

"Satan...!" Randy hissed. Scoffing, "Oh brother—here we go. Here comes the preacher...! I suppose next..., you're gonna tell me frickin' Manning's the antichrist. And then what—we're all going to hell in a handbasket if we don't change our ways?"

Joel didn't respond to Randy's sarcastic jab. There was a part of him that wanted to, but he knew better.

John 3:16-17 *For God so loved the world that He gave His only begotten Son, that whoever believes in Him should not perish but have everlasting life. For God did not send His Son into the world to condemn the world, but that the world through Him might be saved.*

-Chapter Four-
TWO KINDS OF LOVE

If there's anything he's learned over the last twelve years as a Born Again, it doesn't do any good to talk about God, the Bible, or the Gospel of Jesus Christ when emotions are high. It tends to do more damage than good.

Besides, he knows where Randy and even that rude woke-liberal enforcer is coming from; why they take issue with him. Not only that, but they have a good argument. In fact, there was a time when Joel would have argued right alongside them.

The argument really just boils down to two kinds of love. Everyone getting along is one kind of love; the liberal love recited in the lyrics of 'Imagine'; America's new surrogate National Anthem. The other is the love of someone saving another's life; which is the love

DAVID ALAN SMITH

Jesus brought to the table. The problem is, Jesus' definition of saving one's life is saving them from a perilous afterlife.

He came to save, which is really hard to find any hate in that, but people do. Those who abide in his message and share it are hated as well; hated being anything from disliked or politely shunned to all-out resentment. Getting a good dose of the hatred over the last few minutes only served to remind Joel of something else that Jesus brought to the table; division—of which he himself openly said so.

Shockingly, he told his disciples that he didn't come to bring *peace on earth*; that he instead had come to bring division…, '*a sword*' to be precise. He even went so far as to say it would pit family members against family members.

Division can never fit in the liberal's definition of love so eloquently described in 'Imagine'. Love touting unity and world peace can only condemn division. To them it is the antithesis to love; which would be 'hate'. It's why the Liberal villagers are taught to accuse the Jesus Fundamentalists of being haters and dividers. They're branded as being combative, and opposed to world peace and harmony.

The fact of the matter is Jef's want world peace as much as the next guy. They want to get along as much as anyone else. They're however only met with grief;

IT WAS A FREEWILL RAPTURE

laid blamed and shamed for all the evil atrocities committed in the name of Christianity over the course of history.

When Jesus said he came with '*a sword*'; he meant his message wouldn't be received by all people, thus would only end up in division. He didn't mean go out and slay people in his name as in the Crusades, or capture and torture people as they did in the Spanish Inquisition, or execute people as they did in the Salem Witch Trials, or fraudulently bilk money out of the pockets of people — all in the name of Jesus. The Christian cults, along with all those who condemn and threaten people with hellfire and brimstone has never helped the Gospel either. There's a difference between a friendly and compassionate cautionary warning and a fanatical finger-pointing condemnation.

When confronted with these wrongs and injustices; Joel can only shake his head and agree; leaving him with nearly zero room to follow up with a rebuttal. To say these shameful Christian's don't represent Jesus Christ is never enough. When the discussion gets this far into the weeds; to say the love Jesus brought to the table is meant to be lovingly and peacefully shared with others only falls on deaf ears.

The Gospel, meaning 'the good news', was never meant to be jammed down the throats of people or weaponized. That's not what 'good news' is supposed

≈ 39 ≈

to do. It was never intended to threaten or intimidate anyone; let alone invoke war. Nor is it to be utilized as an avenue to get rich or powerful.

It's unfortunate certain people and entities over the course of history failed to understand this. It only leaves one to wonder about the *'powers of darkness'*; Satan being clever enough to even twist the name of Jesus to compel people to do his bidding. If this is the case, one can only admit what a good job he's done.

The bottom line is Joel knows and understands the argument the Liberals have against him — against the Jesus Fundamentalists. He also understands the 'personal peace' argument, an off-shoot to world peace by way of everyone minding their own damn business. This was Joel for the longest time; one who just wants to be left alone — who doesn't want to hear, let alone be told about the love that Jesus brought to the table. In their case, they don't hate the Jef's for being divisive or accuse them of being haters; they hate them for being intrusive; for meddling.

They can be Christian or non-Christian; it doesn't matter — personal peace is personal peace. Having lived the life..., Joel can only agree; 'just leave me alone' is something that is practically impossible to argue with. It's why, in most cases, he doesn't even bother to discuss *'the cross'* with the 'personal peace' folks anymore. Mainly, because he totally gets it.

IT WAS A FREEWILL RAPTURE

He'll mention it, or bring it to their attention with every open window, but that's about it. It's always brief and short, like plucking a tiny seed in loose soil with the hope of another coming along to pour water on it so as to take root and eventually grow. Beyond that, he's left with only one other option; and that is to simply pray for them — that God intervenes and opens their eyes as God opened his.

Still…, even with all this, the question remains as to which of the two kinds of love one chooses to serve. Go with the love that divides by way of trusting the Bible, having faith in what Jesus said…? Or go with the love that doesn't offend anyone; the love that strives for unity and world peace, of which includes personal peace — to be left alone, everyone minding their own business?

Joel already knows for most; the decision is a no-brainer. Who in the world wouldn't love 'world peace' or love to be left alone? Who in the world would want to join a group of people constantly called haters, divisive, annoying and intrusive?

As to whether or not one can go with both kinds of love; secretly clinging to one while pretending to promote the other? The answer is yes; it's a piece of cake. One can easily get away with it. The problem however isn't what one can get away with down here on earth, amongst people. It's what's above

∽ 41 ∽

DAVID ALAN SMITH

they need to consider.

"...whoever denies me before men, I will deny him before my Father in heaven." is just something to fear. It clearly means there are eyes in high places watching.

It goes on to say 'these eyes' see who modifies Jesus. They see all those who conjure up their own versions of Jesus, who alter and edit his gospel and ministry to be more in line with the lyrics of 'Imagine', or whatever else they want him to be. The Jesus-changing Christians are sincere and honest to say they don't and won't deny Jesus, but one needs to ask if it's only because their crafted Jesus obeys them and what they say instead of the other way around. Only God knows.

As for the Jesus Fundamentalists..., they don't alter Jesus or the gospel to condone or accommodate their lifestyles, let alone fit into society. It's why this scripture alone and the fear of it compels them to spurn Truth Neutrality and remain faithful to the Bible's unedited version of Jesus. They fear the 'eyes in high places watching' more than they fear society pressuring them to kowtow to the lyrics of 'Imagine'.

Ultimately, this fear the Jef's have; their fear of denying Jesus before men can only bleed into a fear for those who've complied to Truth Neutrality; even for the sake of just being left alone. The only thing Joel can say to this, or offer to anyone who'd care to listen,

IT WAS A FREEWILL RAPTURE

more so those dearest to him, is you just don't want to die with this indictment over your head—or soul.

A perilous afterlife...? Only time and death will tell. Is it love or hate to share it? Is it intrusive or thoughtful?

At the moment, all these things that Joel has stowed away in his head; it's just too much to say, let alone convey. It's why Joel just clammed up. Thankfully, even though it took a while, Joel's gotten used to all the animosity.

The STATE intimidating him, the Nazis-like liberal enforcer badgering him, his own brother scolding him, friends avoiding him, people making fun of him; none of it was anything new. It isn't to say it didn't bother him though, because it does. But he's grown accustomed to it; to where he just expects it, ignores it and moves on.

His silence however, as usual, spoke volumes to Randy. He knows his brother well enough to know when Joel shuts down, it means 'drop it'. He doesn't want to discuss it any further; and won't for that matter. It didn't take but a handful of seconds for Randy to feel bad. He knew his 'preacher' remark was uncalled for. But tension was high. It's not an excuse, it's just part of the reason why he lost his cool.

Fortunately, Joel's silence worked like a stimulant. It actually calmed Randy down; enough so to collect

DAVID ALAN SMITH

his thoughts and make amends. Besides, he didn't want to end Joel's visit on a bad note. And he knew Joel didn't either. So, to break the ice, Randy decided to voice up in a most silly way; in a way that Joel would know he's just kidding.

In a semi-obnoxious tone..., mimicking a woke liberal flaunting a self-made lisp, "Well..., Mr Sthmarty Pant-sth...! Is-th he? Is-th Lowell Manning the antichris-tht...?" Randy uttered in the most godawful impersonation ever.

Joel, gazing out the window had to snicker — instantly. He didn't even have to look at Randy to know his apology was being offered in a most humorous way.

Still chuckling..., "No..., Manning's not the antichrist." Joel assured. "Trust me, the antichrist won't be that wimpy or stupid. Nor will the people that love the antichrist be as stupid as all these idiots who idolize Manning. Geez..., what a joke!" Joel concluded.

Randy chuckled right back. They both had the same sentiments about America's latest Woke Commander in Chief; Lowell Manning. Needless to say, their mutual feelings for the man were far from flattering.

President Lowell Manning...? A lot could be said about a so-called world leader who daintily bounces down a staircase limp wristed and their hands flopping up and down like a couple of dead fish. To watch

∞ 44 ∞

IT WAS A FREEWILL RAPTURE

him swagger to a podium, cocky and proud, with his chin up and nose in the air; clearly self-absorbed, spoke volumes. He didn't even have to say a word to know he was a full-blown narcissist madly in love with himself. His body language was plenty enough to figure that out.

Joel couldn't help but remember watching him strut out to the mound in New York Stadium to throw the ceremonial first pitch so as to start the World Series several years back. It was just flat out embarrassing. To sit there and watch America's almighty, all-powerful new President on International Television awkwardly and clumsily windup and toss the baseball like a toddler developing their motor skills only to have the baseball land halfway to home plate left a very unsettling image of America's new leadership.

The pathetic feat, even though it was hardly anything to be concerned about, it left a burning impression. Like Randy and Joel, it left many with doubts, uncomfortable and far from feeling safe and secure to say the least. And from the way things are, there was good reason to worry. In fact, they didn't have to look but out their window to know why they had good reason.

Making their way through Carson City, it was impossible not to notice it's long line of slums. Seeing America's new flag waving off in the distance, here

∽ 45 ∽

and there, was totally appropriate for the cesspool that lay beneath it. It was appropriate for the enforcers also; being the same emblem was slapped all over their vehicles, gear, and uniforms.

It's no longer 'Stars and Stripes' that speak for America. It's now the 'Seven Verticals' that holds the crown; seven vertical stripes, different colors depicting the seven liberal tribes of America. Christened by the Democrat Party, the new flag was touted and ordained to undermine the traditional flag. Ultimately, keeping in line with the Cancel-Culture Movement; the new flag was really more about canceling the old flag.

For both Randy and Joel, canceling America clearly had its consequences from what they could see. Cruising along, they quietly gazed at the ragged sections full of empty graffiti-ridden homes, seedy corners, burnt-out buildings, rut-infested roads, crumbling infrastructure, and homeless encampments growing like weeds. Boarded-up doors and windows, broken windows, litter and trash strewn about, pure garbage heaped up in mounds on every street and alleyway…; to see it all, almost like a tour in the drizzling rain made it very ominous.

Joel liked to think the rain was there to cleanse the once charming little town from all the Marxist Engineering the Democrat Party had imposed on it; on all America for that matter. The daydream was

IT WAS A FREEWILL RAPTURE

short-lived though. Randy cut right into the middle of it; pulled Joel right out of his temporary stupor.

For no particular reason other than to make pleasant conversation, "So…! What time is your flight again?" he asked.

Even though both of them knew exactly what time the flight was, Joel went along. Pulling his itinerary out of his pocket and taking yet another gander at it, "Let's see…, Southwest Airlines, Flight 759 Departure from Reno, NV 10:05 AM, Arrival Tucson, AZ 1:15 PM."

"Eh…, we still have plenty of time." Randy affirmed.

Noticing it was the top of the hour; 7:05 AM, Randy went ahead and turned the radio back on to catch the morning show. Liberal talk shows and State propaganda was about the only thing left for serious radio listeners. The once popular conservative talk shows that helped hold America together for so long has long since been banned from the airwaves and internet— 'hate speech'. Besides, it was getting outright dangerous for them, but more so their families.

The mob-mentality on the Left had gotten to be extremely vicious and hostile; to the point of being normal and expected behavior. It was then the Conservative leaning news outlets and radio commentaries came to a screeching halt. Leaving audiences to sit there and listen to sugar-coated monologues by a bunch of woke-liberal talk show hosts suggesting all is well in America didn't make things better. If anything, it made things worse; it was just flat out sickening.

On this particular morning, Randy and Joel were again reminded just how sickening it can be as they begrudgingly forced themselves to listen on.

"Good Morning..., Good Morning..., Good Morning..., America...! And how good America is this fine day." would be the boisterous and chipper announcers inspiring words shouted out to millions of listeners. "I have three words, America; Beau—Ti—Ful...!

Hey, not only in the nation, but right here in beautiful down town Reno, the friendliest city, with the friendliest radio station, KLIF featuring none other than America's friendliest radio talk show host. It's yours truly, me—Sal Salli at your service and here to share the love folks—to share the love."

"Sssss, how sappy is that?" Joel groaned.

It was only because he found Sal Salli's vibrant assessment of America just a little disingenuous; just another fabricated fact the liberals embrace to authenticate their fabricated intelligence. Randy turned to Joel with a countenance that totally agreed with his sarcastic remark. In silence, he went right back to watching the road. Sal Salli however went on with his

IT WAS A FREEWILL RAPTURE

perky upbeat spiel.

"Well ladies, gentlemen, and the gender-select, he's at it again. The news of the morning is big..., B...I...G...G...big! If you haven't heard already, Gaia's Giant— 'Antaeus the Great' —Mother Earth's Champion obviously just can't get enough.

OH...! How I love this man! We all love him! The man is unstoppable, not only in the ring, not only in Hollywood, not only in California, as if being Governor isn't enough; Ezekiel 'Bronze' Solomon is now shooting for, what else...., the Presidency. That's right folks..., you heard right. It's official! California's beloved Governor—Bronze Solomon—has set his sights on being President Manning's successor." Sal excitedly cheered.

"Geez...! What next?" Randy jeered, speaking out of the side of his mouth.

On the same page, "Well..., it looks like we're on our way to another duly selected president from the powers-that-be. Humph..., from a wimpy, little wet rag, mommy's boy to a 7 ½ foot giant; a pro wrestler— only in America." Joel uttered in amazement.

"WHAT...! Are you crazy?" Randy blurted. "Frickin' Manning's not gonna give up his seat on the throne. That mother f—ers' in it for the long run. He's planning on being President until he dies; even then he's probably got a plan up his butt to make that

∽ 49 ∽

DAVID ALAN SMITH

happen as well."

Joel could only smile and chuckle at Randy's political assessment despite the colorful curse words he used to enhance it.

Continuing, "Antaeus the Great...," Randy scoffed shaking his head with a smile, entertaining the thought. "Well at least he's got some balls. Manning..., the little wimp wife of a man is just flat out embarrassing. The guy sucks big time. But, man..., he's a shifty little bastard—I'll give him that."

"Yeah..., well..., wimp or not—the woke-aholics here in Woke-istan love him like he's the purple dinosaur or..., or that spoiled-rotten brat kid whose doting parents will never find any fault in him. But..., sheesh! They love and adore Bronze Solomon too. It'll be interesting to see what happens. I guess we'll see soon enough who the Libs pick to be their loving dictator." Joel surmised.

"You mean..., our dictator." Randy sarcastically reminded.

"Ssss...," Joel hissed, half scoffing and half agreeing with the dismal thought.

Shaking his head, he just sank into his seat and went right back into catching some more of Sal Salli's propaganda; despite how deflating it is.

"And don't forget people, next week is Climate Control Week. The mandatory 'brown-outs' and

IT WAS A FREEWILL RAPTURE

lockdowns here in Reno and Las Vegas are sneaking up on us again — so stalk up on candles, kerosene, and propane. Now…, you don't need me to remind you that Climate Change is still and existential threat to our existence. Right, Beatrice…?"

"That's right Sal." His sidekick sharply agreed with pep. It did indeed resemble a children's show, because of the way they were talking.

"You know it…, I know it…, we all know it. But, having said that, I just have to add folks; how good it feels to know in our hearts that we, the people, as global citizens, together are faithful and true to do our part to save this precious planet of ours. For the children…, right?" he cheered.

"Their future depends on us— 'in us we trust'— you know the mantra. So, folks, let us once again pat ourselves and each other on the back and take a moment to thank ourselves for the sacrifices we make for the sake of peace, security, and the preservation of our home and family — Mother Earth and Humanity."

The propaganda? It wasn't anything Randy or Joel wanted to hear; let alone anything they'd ever agree with. But like yesterday, and the day before, and the day before that — they could only cringe and bear it, but not without grumbling and griping about it for the sake of keeping their sanity intact.

This, they both knew — and knew well.

PART TWO
'…THE RAPTURE…'

Luke 17:26-30 *And as it was in the days of Noah, so it will be also in the days of the Son of Man: They ate, they drank, they married wives, they were given in marriage, until the day that Noah entered the ark, and the flood came and destroyed them all. Likewise, as it was also in the days of Lot: They ate, they drank, they bought, they sold, they planted, they built; but on the day that Lot went out of Sodom it rained fire and brimstone from heaven and destroyed them all. Even so will it be in the day when the Son of Man is revealed.*

Jesus

-Chapter Five-
FREEWILL RAPTURE

Immediately after Sal Salli's syrupy Climate Change spiel; Randy spoke up and Joel was happy for it. Anything but Sal Salli he thought to himself.

"Now tell me the truth…, doesn't that just make you want to puke?" Randy asked, only to get Joel to snicker again. Obviously, they both needed another serious dose of sanity, so in came the complaining Cavalry to save the day.

Jeering, "Frickin' Climate Control…, mandatory

DAVID ALAN SMITH

brown-outs and black-outs, and lockdowns to save the planet," Randy hissed. "What a frickin' joke. It's gotta be the Liberals crown jewel of sanctimonious stupidity. It's right up there with mandatory helmets for toddlers taking baths."

Caught off guard by the snide remark, Joel took his snicker to a full-on laugh. Randy always had a way to make people laugh in spite of serious dialogue.

Still griping, "Man-made Climate Change…, Man-made Climate Change," he mocked with a frantic high pitch voice. "I mean what th' hell? What do these idiots think…, you know? Like what about the Ice Age—it's coming and going? What…, too many cave men, cave women and cave gender-selects roasting too many frickin' marshmallows on too many camp fires melted all the ice and snow? Or maybe too many Mammoths cutting farts—adding to the greenhouse gases? I mean give me a break…!"

"Uhh…, I don't think they had marshmallows back then, Randy." Joel joked, sort of teasing him. Randy responded with a jovial hiss only to hear Joel make another point.

"Besides…, I don't think they even teach kids about the Ice Age anymore because it throws cold water on their man-made climate change narrative. You know how it is—gotta keep 'em stupid to control 'em."

"You know…, I've said it before and I'll say it

IT WAS A FREEWILL RAPTURE

again." Randy said. "The day they started to penalize and arrest people for criticizing all this Manmade Climate Change bullshit was the day America gave in to pure communism. I mean it's weird — they're using a barrel of a gun to force us to say manmade climate change is the truth and not a belief, but here they are with the same gun forcing you to say the Gospel of Jesus is a belief and not the truth."

This time with a sneer of disgust, "Nothing's changed, huh. When it comes to the Left and the Liberal Pharisees, it's always been double standards. Isn't that what you call 'em..., Liberal Pharisee's...?" Randy asked in passing.

"Yeah..., that amongst some other things," Joel said.

"Well..., I call 'em Liberal Nazis-assholes, frickin' idiots, and hypocrites. How's that for love and world peace?" Randy proudly confessed. "I don't know..., like you — they just piss me off."

Joel could only laugh again as they cruised along. The miles came and went as did the minutes. Before they knew it, they were well out of the city and back to taking in the sights of the vast open country. It was actually looking like it was going to be a beautiful day after all; not by Sal Salli's terms, but weatherwise. The drizzling rain had stopped, the clouds broke up and the sun came pouring in to warm things up.

DAVID ALAN SMITH

The timing was perfect because Randy and Joel had come to the end of their little nightmare with DSS and the dismal tour featuring all to the depressing sights in Carson City. To know how welcoming and quaint it used to be bothered them. Randy having pointing out a park where a street preacher was chased down, beat to death, and strung up in a tree made it exceptionally grim. Joel found it disturbing; broke his heart. To think heinous attacks such as this were now pretty common only made it worse.

On a good note, they're past it all now and glad for it. Putting it all behind them was a huge relief. They went back to chatting about this and that; good things because they had their fill of the darker stuff; of which there was just too much of these days. Pleasant conversation was always well received, especially now that they're both in a better mood.

Going on something said on the radio, a commercial regarding some microchip clinic sparked another lighthearted conversation.

"So—are you gonna get chipped?" Randy asked, "they're free."

"Yeah..., right!" Joel scoffed. "Free with our tax money—but nah! There's no way I'm gonna get chipped." Joel assured. "What about you?"

"Nope! These frickin' National ID Cards and facial scans are bad enough. Becky and Jake went ahead

IT WAS A FREEWILL RAPTURE

and had Sean and Skye chipped though. They bought into the GPS stuff, you know, tracking them in case they get lost or kidnapped. So—are they going to go to hell for taking the—what do you call it—the mark of the beast?" Randy asked with a short chuckle and snort.

Joel smiled. He couldn't help but go along with the joke. Mimicking Arnold Schwarzenegger, "Ya..., they'll go straight to hell. The chips need to be surgically removed. Now! We must go back." Joel demanded.

Chuckling, "Hey—that was a pretty good Arnold." Randy praised only to pry a little more into the subject. "So..., uhh..., what is the deal again about the Mark?" he asked. "Cuz, I have a feeling all of us are going to have to take that frickin' chip sooner or later. If we take it, does that mean—you know...?"

"No..., it's not the 'mark of the beast'—if that's what you're asking. It's not to say the 'mark of the beast' won't be a chip though or..., or an embellishment of a chip already implanted. But..., it could be something else too—maybe a tattoo. Whatever it is—one will know it's the mark because it'll come with a pledge of allegiance to the antichrist when you willfully accept it.

When that day comes, you'll have a choice. You either pledge your allegiance and take the mark or get executed—beheaded is what the Bible says. That's the pledge that's gonna seal the fate of people in the end." Joel explained.

"Beheaded? Humph..., crazy—sounds like world peace and love is gonna get a little barbaric." Randy muttered.

"Yeah..., and not only that." Joel added. "All this stuff about not being able to go into stores to buy things, or do things, or..., or get a job or go anywhere without our Vaccine Passports or a facemask whenever they order it; if you think it's bad now—just wait until the 'mark of the beast' hits. This stuff goin' on now isn't the 'mark of the beast', but you could say it's a sort of precursor. You get a pretty darn good idea as to how it'll be; only a thousand times worse. You either starve, get your head cut off, or take the mark?"

"Ni-iiice...!" Randy teased, "Can't wait...! But hey, I got a novel idea. How 'bout we talk about something a little more mysterious and darker instead of all this happy stuff. Say..., your love life? Rumor has it you're still foolin' around with that lady friend of yours? What's her name..., Leah? Do I hear wedding bells?" he teased.

With a cheerful hiss, "No..., no wedding bells. And we're not foolin' around, geez—we never were." Joel clarified. "We're just close, like sister and brother sort of close, you know, Christian fellowship."

IT WAS A FREEWILL RAPTURE

"Well..., how's she doin'? It's Leah..., right? Isn't that her name?"

"Yeah..., Leah..., and she's doin' ok. Still having some issues with her teenage daughter, typical rebellion kind of stuff, but other than that she's doin' just fine. She's a great gal..., witty, and funny, smart..., like you Randy," Joel playfully praised.

Randy rolled into a proud smile accepting the jovial comment like an award. Joel, however did have a little more to share regarding Randy's sneaky inquiry into his personal life.

But—," Joel emphasized, "if you must know, I have been spending a little time with another girl that might..., well maybe tip over to a more romantic side of things."

"Yeah..., what's her name? Is she a Jesus Super-Freak like you and that Leah chick?" Randy asked poking fun.

"Oh..., brother," Joel laughed, "No..., well..., yeah—she's a Jef—used to be Catholic until the State renamed her. But, as for being a Super-Freak—like us? I don't think so—at least not yet, but I'm workin' on it." He joked. "She's new to our group of Born-Agains."

"New..., huh? So, what's her name?" Randy prodded.

"Julie..., Julie Montez. She's cool—became good friends with Leah too. She wanted to go with her to

ᖇ 61 ᖇ

DAVID ALAN SMITH

pick me up at the airport, but chances are she won't be able to because of work."

"Hmmm...," Randy pondered. "Leah..., Julie..., sounds like a couple of pretty nice gals—gotta be the Christian in them..., huh?"

"Oh..., I don't know about that..., don't have to be Christian to be good and decent people. But I will say this about them, especially Leah—we're definitely singing the same tune when it comes to the Bible. She knows her Bible well, and man, we get into some deep Bible talk. You ought to join us some time; we'll zoom it—chat live on line." Joel offered, half-kidding.

"Oh yeah, right..., and put me in a coma? Hell..., no! Not me...! You can keep your Jesus stuff to your-self. Besides, I've heard enough Bible and Jesus crap over the last thirty minutes to last me a life time."

Keeping it jovial, "So..., are you gonna tell your gal-pals about our wild and crazy party and how much fun we had?" Randy asked.

"Party..., what party?"

"You know..., the party we had with DSS. Are you gonna tell 'em about that Enforcer doing a table dance for you, how you were stuffing twenty-dollar bills in his leopard-skin G-string and gun holster?"

"You're funny," Joel countered, "you're just full of jokes today, aren't you? But, yeah..., I'll tell them. Leah's actually going through the same thing I am.

IT WAS A FREEWILL RAPTURE

The Woke Gestapo is after her too. Julie just had her first roadside inquisition the other day. Leah's like on her fourth. Both of them say they're not gonna comply though. But who knows…? It's frickin' tough—the pressure. I just about broke back there." Joel confessed.

"Man…, it really sucks what they're doin' to you guys." Randy empathized.

"Yeah…, I know. It's only a matter of time before we're taken to the Camp. I don't know. I just don't want to think about it right now. Right now, I'm thinkin' it'll be good to get back home and settle in—get back into the swing of things."

The conversation went quiet for the moment. Even though Joel's remark was geared to be on a positive note, it was somber. They both knew what was coming and it was depressing; even scary.

Despite what Joel said, he didn't go into thinking about how good it'll be to get home. Instead, he went directly into thinking about getting his affairs in order before the State hauls him away to the Sensitivity Camp. He was sure to lose everything he owned. He began to contemplate as to what, and to who, and when he's to give his belongings away before the State gets their hands on them. After a minute or so, Randy broke the somber silence.

"Well, little brother, I hate to say it, but this'll probably be the last time you'll ever get to ride in ol' Blue."

Speaking of his truck.

Joel started to answer him, but he didn't get but two words in when it happened.

BAM....! BOOM...!

Out of nowhere a loud and thunderous shot of lightening cracked across the sky; from the east to the west. It startled them, even jolted them. If the seatbelts weren't on, they probably would have crashed into the roof of the cab.

It was powerful; like a massive sonic-boom. Immediately, within seconds it went dark, like an eclipse; like something placed in front of the sun. It wasn't clouds, or smoke..., it was more like a huge blanket..., a sort of veil.

In the same moment, the truck came to an abrupt standstill, so did the oncoming traffic. They didn't come to a rolling stop; it was instant—as fast as a car hitting a wall, but it wasn't like that. There was no impact of a crash or collision. It was as if they were grabbed by something; grabbed from behind by a giant and held in place—like a cat catching an unsuspecting mouse on the move. The motor kept running, but only at an idle. Randy's foot pressing down hard on the gas pedal had no effect whatsoever.

Like the cars, Randy too was pinned to the seat, he couldn't move. He yelled and tried to look over at Joel but couldn't turn his head. He was like frozen in place.

IT WAS A FREEWILL RAPTURE

Looking straight ahead, he could see the oncoming traffic and was able to look in his rearview mirror.

He could see that all the other cars had stopped as well, in front of him and behind him. Nothing was moving. The cars closest to him, he was able enough to see the people inside them as well. It was however just a mirror image. They too were pinned in place like he was; consumed by fear and screaming for dear life.

Joel was however in a different state. He was free. He was shaking and trembling, but he was free to move about. Things were going down, things he never expected, but nevertheless going down. He looked over at Randy, frozen in place, pinned, and panicking.

He quickly scooted over, grabbed his arm and carefully tugged on him. He was gentle at first, but it didn't take but a handful of seconds before Joel was pushing and pulling as hard as he could to shake him loose, but it was no use. Randy was just flat out stuck right where he sat.

It became really clear, real fast, there was nothing he could do for Randy. He knew it, he just knew it. Joel heard the voices. Randy could hear them too, but was too freaked out to understand them. Joel, on the other hand, could. As soon as he heard them, and what they were saying, he knew it was time; time to go and time to leave Randy in God's hands.

Having already pulled back in defeat, he again

DAVID ALAN SMITH

reached over and put his hand on top of Randy's right hand white-knuckling the steering wheel. "This is it, Randy. It's time. I've gotta go." Joel explained.

Randy, wide-eyed with fear again started yelling, not knowing what was happening. He wasn't in pain; he just couldn't move.

"Randy..., Randy...!" Joel yelled so as to overpower Randy's panic. "Listen to me..., I'm going now. I've gotta go. I love you. Tell Rebecca I love her too. Listen, my Bible, get my Bible. It's in my suitcase. Get it. I put something in there for you guys," he clamored.

He then took a quick glance around at everything going on. He was in awe and excited. By this time, a most wonderful and sweet-smelling aroma had filled the air; it was so alluring, almost trancing.

The feeling that consumed him wasn't at all fear though; quite the opposite. It was bliss; indescribable bliss that had Joel floating on the edge of euphoria. The voices he was hearing were so beautiful and inviting. To say they were comforting would better describe it.

Joel turned back to Randy and bid him farewell one last time. It wasn't slow and sentimental, far from sappy. It was fast and short..., pressing and hasty.

"I'll see you, Randy. I'll see you. Take heed, cling to Jesus and..., well..., just 'believe God'." He pleaded loudly and firm. "You gotta believe Him, Randy." He took one last sentimental glance at his brother in

IT WAS A FREEWILL RAPTURE

silence, a mere second and blurted, "Man…, I gotta go — I gotta go…, Godspeed!"

With that, he turned, scooted and shuffled out the passenger door. Strangely enough, despite the frantic good-bye, Joel's departure out the door wasn't hurried. It was casual, even calm; like he was being gently escorted.

Randy, out of the corner of his eye, was able to see Joel slide out of the truck and walk off towards something. A light, a vision, he couldn't quite tell. Grunting and straining, he struggled to wiggle free or at least turn his head, but it was no use. As for Joel, it wasn't but seconds before Randy could see that his brother was gone.

Suddenly, as quickly as it came, the overpowering invisible restraints, whatever it was holding everything in place, let loose. The truck and the vehicles snapped back into motion like a stubborn, rusty bolt cracked loose by a wrench.

Randy and the other drivers nearly collided as they quickly found themselves managing their vehicles instantly moving again at full speed. Jerking and pulling, they swerved past each other. The cars in back of him weren't so lucky. It wasn't a head on collision, but a collision no less.

Right away, cars pulled over as they regained control of not only their cars, but themselves. By this time, the instant darkness that fell upon them was already gone as if it never went dark in the first place. The sweet mesmerizing aroma? Gone, leaving nothing but gusty winds in its place.

Slamming his truck to a stop, Randy immediately jumped out and started to race back to where Joel disappeared but didn't get more than three or four yards before he was abruptly shaken and knocked off balance by a short rigid earthquake. Stumbling and nearly falling to the ground, "What the…?" he cursed. And cursed again.

Rattled, he instinctively adjusted to stabilize himself; only to pause and halfway anticipate another tremor. Sure enough. A second, but mild rumble danced beneath his feet. It was nowhere near the jolt of the first, but it was no less intimidating.

A couple of seconds at most however was plenty enough time to absorb the quakes before Randy launched another sprint to where Joel and that light thing was. Getting there, he yelled and yelled for him. There was nothing, so it seemed.

There on ground, was Joel's clothes; strewn about and rolling with the sweeping wind. His pants, shirt and shoes, everything he was wearing was there, but no Joel. Randy buckled to his knees, frantically looking down and around, and sifting through Joel's clothes he panicked even more.

IT WAS A FREEWILL RAPTURE

He'd run his hand over his head in bewilderment and confusion; wondering what was going on. There was really nothing to go on. He didn't know what to do.

He heard some hollering and a ruckus within earshot of where he planted himself. It was coming from the other drivers, coming from where the crash was.

"Where's my baby? SARAH...!" came wailing out of the mix; that and some carrying on about a glowing orb sweeping in and out of the mothers car. Apparently, it swiped the little child right out of the car seat.

Wasting no time, Randy jumped up and ran over to them, not only to help them, but to find out about Joel. Maybe he was over there. He didn't know.

Running into the heart of the small gathering, he'd be stopped short. Grabbing Randy's arm, "Did you see it," one of them asked all wound up. It was a middle-aged woman about his age.

"What," Randy asked. "See what?"

"The stairs..., the light..., that guy..., that guy in your truck. He just walked into it and he was gone," she hysterically ranted.

"Walked into what?"

"I don't know, but I saw it. I saw something like..., like a glowing doorway and..., and stairs..., I don't know, something weird. That guy in your

DAVID ALAN SMITH

truck, he just got out like he was holding someone's hand and walked into it and…, and he was gone. All of it, it all disappeared — except for his clothes. They just came floating down to the ground from…, I don't know — maybe twenty, thirty feet up. It was right in front of me, I saw it." She clamored, clearly shaken up.

Randy just looked at her. He didn't know how to answer her let alone what to ask. He was totally dumbfounded. It didn't take but a second to be drawn back to the commotion though; back to the crowd and the woman desperately carrying on about her missing daughter. He hustled in to see if he could assist in any way, but clearly there wasn't anything there for him to do, except freak out along with them.

Everybody was in shock, squabbling as to what had just happened and tending to the injured and the raving woman. Three people were injured, but not seriously. The front of their SUV clipped the back side of a runaway car that swerved across the lane in front of them. It sat upside down about forty feet away. It was a little Toyota Corolla, an older model twisted and mangled up from the collision and rolling over several times.

Yelling back, "There isn't any driver! The driver's gone!" was the standout words that came out of the group tending to the Corolla.

70

IT WAS A FREEWILL RAPTURE

Hearing that surely didn't help matters. It only added to the chaos and confusion. It was like throwing gas on the fire already burning out of control. And that fire would be the hysteria.

Amos 5:18-19 *"Woe to you who desire the day of the Lord!*

For what good is the day of the Lord to you? It will be darkness, and not light.

It will be as though a man fled from a lion; And a bear met him! Or as though he went into the house, Leaned his hand on the wall; And a serpent bit him!"

-Chapter Six-
LIONS, COYOTES AND BIRDS

The buzz was ablaze. Everyone was going back and forth about the bizarre standstill, the quake, and the missing girl. Like Joel, the only thing left of her was her clothes scattered about outside of the car and a doll she had in her arms.

People were searching the premises for both the little girl and the driver of the Corolla, but they were nowhere to be found. In the mix was a young man, early twenties or so; a kid from Randy's perspective who kept on insisting that the woman driving the Corolla was gone because she disappeared.

Randy heard him telling others the very same

IT WAS A FREEWILL RAPTURE

thing that the lady was describing to him. The only difference is he kept on insisting it was UFO's and aliens; that she was abducted — and the little girl too.

Randy quickly went up to him, "Where...?" he asked. "Where did she disappear?"

He pointed, "Back there."

"Please, please show me" Randy pleaded.

Ditching the ruckus, the two of them hurriedly jogged back down the road, to where the kid thought he saw the woman get out of her car. It was about sixty yards or so, considering the car rolled a certain distance before the collision itself. In between his huffs and puffs as they hurried along, the kid kept on about the lady walking over to the glowing door and seemingly up some stairs, is how he put it.

As they neared and came to a halt, catching their breath, "There...! Right there!" the kid said, pointing to the spot.

"Oh no...," Randy groaned and started running ahead.

The kid just looked at him and followed. He really didn't see what Randy had already spotted. It was her clothes. They too lay scattered about; lifeless, if not for the wind trying to dislodge them from the brush and branches.

"Oh, God..., oh no," Randy spoke out loud. "I don't believe it..., no way."

DAVID ALAN SMITH

"What…?" the kid asked.

"It was the Rapture." Flustered and nervous, "The Rapture, it was the Rapture…, the Bible, you know, the Bible, the Christians…!" Randy tried to convey.

It was pointless. The kid didn't know what he was talking about. He did however know all about the prize laying there in the midst of the ladies' belongings. He quickly bent down and picked up a beautiful gold diamond ring. He shuffled the clothes a little more and found a gold necklace as well.

"What are you doing?" Randy snapped at the kid to confront him.

Defensive, cocky and shrugging, "I don't know…, she's gone. I may as well have 'em. There's no sense in leaving 'em here." the kid justified as he slipped the treasures into his pocket. "I mean…, if she comes back or we find her, I'll give them back," he assured.

Thinking it wrong, shaking his head, half surprised and half disappointed, "Jeez…," Randy questioned. For a second, it bothered him to see how the kid was so easily lured away from everything going on with a couple pieces of jewelry.

"What….?" the kid barked to challenge Randy's scrutiny.

"Never mind," Randy said as he turned to scamper back to get Joel's things left on the ground. He took a couple of steps and froze. He stopped dead in

IT WAS A FREEWILL RAPTURE

his tracks. Caught off guard, both he and the kid were met with a very unwelcoming sight.

"What the hell…?" the kid uttered as he tensed up.

About fifty feet or so, pacing back and forth was a small pack of coyotes; six, seven, nine or ten. It was hard to tell and counting them was the last thing on their mind. They were off to the side a bit but sneaked in far enough to cut them off from heading back to the scene of the accident.

Randy and the kid remained perfectly still. Leery and unsure; they just stared at the unpredictable gang of wild canines. The coyotes didn't appear to be scared, hesitant maybe, but not scared. They didn't even look curious. They looked dangerous and they were dangerously close.

"What do we do?" the kid nervously whispered.

"Don't move," was about all Randy could think of saying without really knowing what to do.

Yelping and snarling like hyenas, they seemed to be anticipating as to whether or not to attack. One would dart in a couple of feet, but stop short, then another, and another, then two as if they were taking turns, taunting each other to be the first to go in for the kill.

Randy could see a couple of them were foaming at the mouth. He was scared, really scared. He felt defenseless; a horrible feeling—one he's never

DAVID ALAN SMITH

experienced until now.

He quickly scoured his surroundings in search of a branch, rocks; anything he thought he could use to at least try and fight them off if they attack — but there was nothing. Locking his eyes back on the imminent danger gripped him; enough to even take his mind off what had just happened with Joel and everything else going on. It all vanished for the moment. Right now, it was him and his young guide facing off with these rabid coyotes that mattered, nothing else.

Suddenly, hearing a car come up the road from behind them, the kid instantly turned around and took off running towards it away from the threat. His mad dash was enough to trigger the coyotes, they immediately charged. With the kid high-tailing it, leaving Randy there to confront the coyotes on his own, Randy didn't hesitate.

He reacted and reacted fast. He took off running as well, but off to the side going across the road. Thankfully the car had already slowed down trying to figure out what was up with the kid. The coyotes split as they neared them. Of the bunch, only one went after Randy, the rest raced towards the kid banging on the windows of the car.

Randy could hear him yell. "Let me in, let me in," he screamed. "Please…!" The people in the car wouldn't be so kind. It wasn't but seconds before the

IT WAS A FREEWILL RAPTURE

raving coyotes would catch up and mercilessly attack without reservation. As for the car, it sped off.

Randy already on the other side of the road turned on the lone coyote as it grabbed him by the heel. He'd fall to the ground, turn and start kicking for dear life. Kicking, and kicking, yelling and using his fist to fight off his attacker was the only thing he could do. It worked. After a handful of seconds, thirty seconds maybe, the coyote dashed off to join his gang of killers.

By this time, the kid's blood-curdling screams were over. They didn't last long once the larger part of the pack caught up to him and ripped him apart. He tried to run and even made it over an embankment into a ditch, but that was it.

It was a horrible sound. It bothered Randy. Even though it was over quickly and already running back to the crowd as fast as he could, he could still hear the screams echoing in his head. The crowd had also heard it off in the distance, but couldn't really make out what was going on.

Looking on, they saw Randy running towards them. As he came up, he paused and cautiously looked back to see if there was any more danger in pursuit of him. Gasping, out of breath, hunched over with his hands clinching his knees he'd address the curious on-lookers now wondering what else could possibly be going on.

DAVID ALAN SMITH

Heavily panting and out of breath, "There's a..., a pack of..., a pack of rabid coyotes back there," he said, struggling with every word.

Continuing, "They attacked us. They attacked us and that kid..., that kid that was with me," he said. "They killed him. You gotta get out of here," Randy warned.

The small crowd started mumbling, but for the most part, Randy was met with the 'deer in the headlight' kind of response. He then looked around for the car that abandoned the kid, but it was nowhere in sight. It kept on going, even past the scene of the accident.

He was furious. He wanted to confront them, give them a piece of his mind for their callous act, but the whole thing was squashed being they were long gone. It was just as well, he supposed. With everything else going on, scolding a bunch of strangers would only make things worse. He didn't need any more grief as it was.

Figuring there was really no use in staying, he started to run back to his truck, so as to get the heck out of there. He didn't get more than thirty feet though, when he heard a loud screech and scream.

A large hawk of all things, actually a hawk and an owl, in broad daylight no less, came swooping down on the crowd; clearly an attack. The owl however

∽ 78 ∽

IT WAS A FREEWILL RAPTURE

missed its target, an older man in the mix, who managed to duck and bat the owl away. The hawk though, it didn't miss. It managed to sink its talons deep in the backside of a woman's head and neck. It was actually the gal carrying on about her missing daughter. With its majestic wings flapping, and its screeching call of the wild, it was only the woman's screams that had any chance of topping the ferocious sound of the attack.

The onlookers, including Randy, did everything they could to fight it off. Finally, it just soared off into the vast sky. They all kept an eye on it, as well as an eye for anymore birds of prey. It wasn't until they all agreed the coast was clear that they went back to the initial nightmare seemingly getting more and more ominous.

The wind had kicked up a notch and the clouds started thickening up again. It only made the little voice in Randy's head that much louder, "You gotta get out of here."

Looking around, and more than convinced his assistance wasn't needed amongst the gathering, he was again off to the truck. Running back, he instantly went right back to thinking about Joel, how he just disappeared—and how it all happened. With that, he needed to make one more stop. On the side of the road, where Joel vanished, Randy quickly started to gather

DAVID ALAN SMITH

up everything that was left of him. But, even something as simple as that had its dangers.

As he did so, he kept a sharp eye out for anymore rabid coyotes or ravenous birds. But again, the unexpected caught him by surprise. Off in the distance, he could see two mountain lions slowly making their way towards him. He was sure of it; he could clearly make them out—they were lions. They weren't running, but the fact of them heading his way was enough to put him on edge.

He was sure there were at least two, but he wasn't foolish enough to think it was only two—not after all that's happened. Nor was he foolish enough to deny the possibility of others lurking about being much closer than the ones off in the distance.

"Holy s—t...!" He clamored.

With his heart pounding and adrenaline bursting, just like his ordeal with the coyotes; he hurriedly picked up the last of Joel's clothing and raced back to the safety of ol' Blue. Getting there, he tossed Joel's stuff into the cab as he slipped into the driver's seat and slammed the door shut.

His phone sitting on the dash was the first thing that caught his eye. He was so fixated on all the stuff that happened, and happened so fast, that he didn't even think about grabbing it as he rushed back to find Joel and join the commotion.

IT WAS A FREEWILL RAPTURE

It didn't matter though. From what he gathered from the crowd in all its hysteria; nobody's phone was working; no signal. They were all dead; no calls in, no calls out, no 911, or anything else. Communications were cut off; period. For how long; nobody knew any more than why and how it was cut off in the first place. Still, Randy couldn't help but try. He made a few efforts, 911, calling his sister Becky and Jake—nothing but static.

Annoyed, "F this," he said, throwing it down on the seat.

He stared the truck, made a speedy U-turn and made for home; back to South Lake Tahoe. But he slammed on the brakes and came to a screeching halt. He was torn. There was a part of him that felt he needed to stay there and look or even wait for Joel. Again, he just didn't know what to do.

He screamed as if he was in pain. "What do I do? What to do," he raged.

In the immediate silence after his cry, he could hear the radio was still on, but it was just buzzing with static. Sal Salli was nowhere to be found. He turned the dial to see if anything would come through. Maybe there'd be some answers, some updates, anything, but like his phone it proved to be totally useless. Harshly, he turned it off. He took a few moments to make a decision. It didn't take long. It was time to move.

∞ 81 ∞

DAVID ALAN SMITH

He crept up to the scene of the accident, where the gathering was and frantically warned them about the mountain lions. He managed to get past that, but only to be taken back to where the kid was killed. His stomach went sour and cramped up as he approached the spot where the kid desperately raced over the top of the embankment and into the ditch, or gully, where he met his demise.

Randy didn't even want to imagine the grisly mess left at the scene of the beast's crime. It wouldn't however be enough to squelch the haunting screams now planted in his memory. He felt bad, really bad for the kid. So much so that he was tempted to stop and tend to him. But logic won. It got the best of him, but not without getting him angry.

It pissed him off because there was a time when he wouldn't have thought twice about doing it, but that was when it was legal to carry a gun…, and plenty of bullets. His pistol used to be readily available, as he got in the habit of taking it with him when ever he'd leave his home, but no more.

"Frickin' Liberals…!" he cursed under his breath as the thought crossed his mind. It wasn't anything to dwell on, that's for sure. The scathing remark came and went. Still, though only for a moment…, it irked him that he didn't have a gun…, but more so why he didn't.

IT WAS A FREEWILL RAPTURE

He ultimately realized there was nothing he could do — and the coyotes were still out there. Seeing the mountain lions didn't help either. He figured he'd just report it when the phones were back up and running; soon he hoped.

Right now, he just needed to get back home. He stepped on it. His thoughts, racing as fast as his truck, would race through his head as he sped along. There were just so many things to think about.

At the moment; the only thing he knew was he just didn't know. He didn't know what to expect, what was ahead of him, or even if he'd make it back. Where's Joel? Was it over? Those coyotes, and those birds, and mountain lions — how weird? Is there more to come? Was it the Rapture? Was it something else?

It was so overwhelming…: everything. Everything that had just happened, all within thirty minutes would take Randy nearly over the edge; enough to challenge his sanity. But he wasn't the only one.

Far be it.

Luke 17:31-36 *"In that day, he who is on the housetop, and his goods are in the house, let him not come down to take them away. And likewise, the one who is in the field, let him not turn back. Remember Lot's wife. Whoever seeks to save his life will lose it, and whoever loses his life will preserve it. I tell you, in that night there will be two men in one bed: the one will be taken and the other will be left. Two women will be grinding together: the one will be taken and the other left. Two men will be in the field: the one will be taken and the other left."*

Jesus

-Chapter Seven-
AMIELIA, AMIELIA

In a modest two-bedroom upstairs apartment tucked in the heart of Tucson, AZ; Leah would find herself on her knees sobbing to no end. In the middle of her living room floor, on her knees one minute, and the next she'd be laying facedown clawing the carpet in a desperate attempt to grasp it in utter despair.

She would find no comfort. There would be no comfort, no comfort at all. The minutes would pass, and like a wounded and dying animal, she'd once

IT WAS A FREEWILL RAPTURE

again scrounge up just enough strength to drag herself across the floor in search of something…, anything.

She really didn't know where she was going, let alone where to go. Inching her way, weeping and crawling without any direction, without a compass, it would be her bedside where she'd finally end up this time around. Using the sheets, blankets and spread, anything she could cling to, she lifted herself up to her knees once again. Proving to be as repetitive as a broken record, Leah would again scream in agony.

Boiling with rage she'd yell in anger and shoot her rattled thoughts off in every direction. She wanted HIM to hear. She wanted HIM to know just how furious and broken she was. And as the broken record of emotion moved around, she would find herself right back where she started, exhausted and hoarse. She'd cower and collapse, she'd bury her face in the sheets, only to whimper, sob and plead one more time.

"Oh Lord…, LORD…please…, please don't leave me," she'd softly beg.

It would however be to no avail. Her sad predicament was sure and there was no reversing it. Leah had missed the Rapture.

By her side, mildly impaired with marijuana and the residue of an all-night drinking binge is her daughter, Nicki Dawn; who's just short of seventeen years old. To her credit, she had stepped out of her hateful

DAVID ALAN SMITH

and unruly character long enough to actually console her mother for the first time in her young adult life. Being nothing but trouble and a painful heartache for Leah over the last six years, Nicki was suddenly taken in with compassion and sympathy towards her mother.

It would be the first time since she was a child. Hardly remembered; a precious, young, naïve, but sensitive and insightful little child holding her mother, softly and gently rocking back and forth, it would be Nicki as early as three years old who'd take it upon herself to comfort her hurting mom over the years.

Unstable, living from room to room and back to the car again, round and round they went. It was rough. Leah was quite successful when it came to losing jobs and establishing abusive relationships.

Being formally introduced to every insecurity, every snare, every trial and hardship that comes with a young and reckless single mother's legacy, it would be Nicki Dawn helping her face and endure the onslaught of all her mistakes. Leah would eventually clean up and get her life somewhat together, but Nicki had fallen away; drugs, alcohol, promiscuity, defiant, heartless, Godless…, the works.

The warm and sentimental relationship in their early years, being an essential part of their survival had disappeared with Nicki's loss of innocence. Leah's

∞ 86 ∞

IT WAS A FREEWILL RAPTURE

concerted efforts to mend and smooth out their indifferences were futile. Nicki would shun her mom's conciliatory gestures over the years.

She had a new life, a life that Leah knew well. The old adage, "the apple doesn't fall far from the tree" would once again prove to be true. It's been a harsh and abrasive relationship that worsened by the day. Nicki kept it cold and distant. She glamorized her defiance and more often than not, she'd fan the flames.

Still, Nicki would set it all aside when she saw her mom howling in despair after the Rapture. She'd kneel by her grieving mother. She'd silently caress her back and stroke her long dark hair now horribly disarrayed. She would attempt to wipe Leah's swollen and tear-stricken face with a cool damp washcloth every chance she'd get. She'd hold her, she'd softly and gently rock with her like she used to when she was that precious little child. She'd cry with her.

Yes, Nicki too would be crying. She was again, naïve and really unable to fully understand her mother's anguish as she was so many times before as a child dealing with her mother's grief. But, like then, she knew something was horribly wrong. She knew her brokenhearted mom of seventeen long years needed her more now than ever before.

This time however would be different. It was much more than just being there. As tough, strong willed and independent and even invincible as Nicki made herself out to be with all of her godless friends and Chad, her likeminded boyfriend, she found out quickly just how vulnerable and frail she truly is. In the past it was always all about being there for her mom, but this time she found herself needing her mom just as much as her mom needed her.

What happened to Nicki during the Rapture was quite sobering to say the least. Like many, it slapped the stupid, and the defiance and the arrogance right out of her. On one hand, the imprint of the slap turned her into a scared little girl trembling with fear and uncertainty. On the other hand, though, it turned her back into the greatest, most tender loving daughter any mother could ever ask for.

The soft, soothing words and heartfelt apologies Nicki speaks are as beautiful and kind as it gets. Affectionately holding her mother in her arms, doing her best to console her was touching because it was honest and pure. The love pouring out of her was genuine. It however wasn't but an hour ago that Nicki was singing a different tune. And it was an ugly, hateful and selfish tune.

The tune could easily be called 'Once Again'. Once again, Nicki had come staggering into the apartment half lit and half asleep. It was again in the middle of the week. It was again right on schedule; in the morning

IT WAS A FREEWILL RAPTURE

right before her mother would have to shuffle off to work. It was the same ol' approach driven by the same ol' need.

Nicki would politely ask her mother for more money; money so she could do it all again. Leah would once again be reluctant. Leah would once again point out how wrong it was for Nicki to be doing what she was doing. And once again, Nicki would erupt and the war would start.

This particular morning was no different. Back and forth they went; five minutes or so. Getting louder and louder and more and more toxic and fierce, Leah would have to back down.

She so hated to hear Nicki's foul mouth. Hurling vulgar insults and hostile threats every other word was so unbecoming for such a pretty young girl. It just gets to be too much for Leah. The truth is, more often than not, Leah would give in just so she didn't have to see this ugly and vicious side of Nicki.

Finally, after having her fill of the venom; Leah grabbed Nicki's Transfer Card, added another hundred bucks from the DTA (Debit Transfer App) and tossed it on the coffee table. Just like before, and the time before that, and the time before that; it was more about shutting Nicki up with appeasement than an act of kindness on Leah's part.

Nicki took the beefed-up card in a huff and

⮑ 89 ⮐

stormed off to her room so as to gather some things. Leah on the other hand would sit down and catch her breath. Strangely enough, Leah had learned to calm down rather quickly after her coarse confrontations with Nicki and her raucous behavior. It would be the inner peace and joy she had come to know so well. Forgiving; both forgiving and forgetting would be a huge part of the inner peace she found in Christ.

Seeing so much of herself in Nicki, the feisty, independent fireball she once was, she couldn't help but modestly shake her head and let out a halfhearted chuckle. It was enough to shrug off the heated argument, and even smile. She loved Nicki so much. That she knew, and wouldn't change it for the world.

As any loving mother would, she worried about her too. In turn, she prayed for her. Without ceasing, she prayed fervently in light of how wicked, unstable, and dark the world had become; more especially over the last decade. And Nicki, her precious little girl was dancing right smack dab in the middle of it.

After packing a few things to see her through another unsavory adventure, Nicki came stomping out of her bedroom. Cold as steel, unapologetic, and without remorse she made a beeline to the kitchen, totally ignoring Leah pleasantly sitting there on the couch finishing her coffee. Rigid and brisk, she stuffed her backpack with some drinks and snacks, zipped it up

IT WAS A FREEWILL RAPTURE

and headed for the door; already planning to slam it shut on her way out—without any kind of good-bye no less.

And then it happened—

Right out of the blue, out of nowhere; it happened as it did with Randy and Joel hundreds of miles away.

It was a loud boom. Even from inside the apartment, in broad daylight, it was quite easy to assume a blasting flash of lightening had speedily shot out across the sky. Instantly it was dark. Instantly, a loud rumbling voice, shouts and trumpets in the near distance rang out like thunder. And instantly, and more importantly, Nicki was stopped dead in her tracks halfway to the front door. Just like Randy, she couldn't move.

"MOM..., MOM...!" she frantically yelled as loud as she could.

"I..., I can't move! I can't move...! Mom...! MOOOOOMM!" she screamed in utter fright as she tried to squirm and break away from whatever was holding her. She could feel the hands. She could feel the weight, so much weight. Oh, how she struggled to lift her feet and move her arms. It was all she could do to just turn her head, even then it was ever so slight.

Leah, on the other hand, like Joel was as free as a bird. Nothing would be restraining her; nothing at all. After rapidly sitting up and regaining her composure,

∞ 91 ∞

DAVID ALAN SMITH

coffee all over her and shaking from the blast, she quickly stood up in shock.

The first thing she focused on was Nicki, but her natural instinct to rush over to help her was interrupted. It was that quick, Leah was hit by the revelation—it's the Rapture. She knew; just like Joel, she knew it.

The darkness was already lit up with shimmering lights and the room was filled with a most indescribable sweet fragrance when Leah was overwhelmed with a euphoric sensation. It was a magnificent, tingling feeling; it consumed her from head to toe. Her senses were magnified and her instincts were heightened. Undone and overcome by its glory, even though she knew it was benevolent, she'd immediately fall face down in reverence and fear. It was that powerful.

The heavenly voices, the inviting aura, and glowing orbs frolicking and zipping about like fireflies made the spectacle that much more spectacular. Leah was still prone, face down on the floor, but Nicki could clearly see. There was a door that manifested in the midst; a translucent doorway not more than six or seven feet away from her mom.

It was stunning and brilliant; shining gold, silver and glimmering diamonds. It was so bright, but blinding, it was not. There would be a foyer just inside the doorway and a radiant stairway clearly leading up. It wouldn't be until Leah heard the heavenly voices that

∞ 92 ∞

IT WAS A FREEWILL RAPTURE

she would slowly look up and see everything Nicki was seeing.

"Amielia, Amielia…, don't be afraid. Do not fear. Come." was the beautiful voice upon voices beckoning her, calling her. It wasn't her name, but for some reason Leah recognized it. She knew it was her they were calling. It was so wonderful and so alluring. The fear in Leah did indeed dissipate, in fact almost instantly. It vanished and it would be replaced with mesmerizing ecstasy.

She felt a warm hand tenderly slip into the palm of her hand and gently clasp it. It was so soft and graceful; having a sort of sensation about it. A translucent figure gradually stemmed from the hand; materialized into a body. No details, just a radiant and glowing body of light.

Leah could sense it was clearly an angel. It lovingly lifted her arm so as to raise her to her knees and onto her feet. Not wanting to tarry, the graceful and saving angel by the hand would gently tug her so as to lead her to and through the golden doorway, into the foyer and up the stairs.

"Come, Amielia! Come…, it is time. Come with us. Do not be afraid," would peacefully yet persistently invite her.

Leah was so taken in by the Glory; so much so that Nicki's maniacal screams had become faint, even

∽ 93 ∾

distant, but not gone by any means. Starstruck, but far from hypnotized, Leah wanting more than anything to go with the beautiful angel would begin to mosey towards the doorway. It wasn't a question of being coerced, because she was more than alert to know she could stay if she so desired.

Her sense of freewill was not infringed upon, and she knew it. She could feel it. She knew this moment was a benign open-arms invitation; as opposed to a mafia-like offer she can't refuse or a temptation. She knew she could stay, it's just that she didn't want to. There was just something about the voice of Jesus and the hand of an angel welcoming you into the Kingdom of God. Still, Nicki screaming for dear life was giving the Glory of God a run for its money.

"MOOOOOMM...!" would screech across the room. Nicki's frantic screaming wasn't letting up.

At first, Leah wasn't receptive, but with each passing step towards the doorway came another dose of doubt. Feeling the hesitation, the heavenly voices and angels reassured Leah that the Lord would look after Nicki, to just trust HIM. It was so comforting to hear that, yet it was so hard to digest.

"HELP...! MOOOOOMM...! MOOOOOMM...! HELP ME...! PLEEEEASE..., MOM! HELP MEEEEE," Nicki cried with everything she had.

This time it would be enough to get Leah to stop.

IT WAS A FREEWILL RAPTURE

She was already through the door, in the foyer, with one foot on the stairs even, when she would modestly turn around. The voices, pleading with Leah doubled down. They urged her, begged her and encouraged her to just trust the Lord, that He'll take care of Nicki.

Leah could feel it was actually more than just words. She knew that it was a promise, straight from Jesus—but the world took her. She looked back inside the apartment. She'd see her daughter calling to her, so she made the decision.

Leah let go of the angelic hand and hurriedly rushed right out of the translucent foyer straight back into the living room; back to Nicki. She'd grab her; she'd pull her, and push her; the whole time thinking she'd break Nicki loose and take her along with her. As the seconds passed, Leah desperately wrestled with the invisible bindings and weights. She was doing everything she could and as fast as she could to free the one of whom she loves so much.

By this time, Nicki Dawn was bawling uncontrollably. She'd grunt and groan trying ever so hard to twist and turn so as to assist her mom anyway she could to break free. It was the Hand of God that they were trying to loosen, and it was clearly useless. They were powerless. Nicki wasn't budging. Still, the both of them tried with all their might.

The voices would keep beckoning, "Amielia,

come—it is time."

Eventually, the passing moments delivered the last call. Leah, of course had no idea there'd be a last call. Nor did she acknowledge when the voices went silent. She was far too preoccupied to pay any attention. She just needed a couple more seconds, that's all; just a few more seconds.

Fixated and determined, Leah lodged herself under the backpack strapped over Nicki's shoulders. She firmly planted her feet and with vigor and oomph, like trying to topple a three-ton statue, she pushed and strained as hard as she could to bust Nicki out of her standstill. And with a blast of a trumpet, a flash of light and a deafening thud, the Rapture was over—just like that.

As fast as a light switch turning off a light; Nicki's binding instantly ended with a snap in the same way Randy, and Randy's truck did. Leah and Nicki shot across the room like a rubber band only to slam into the front door; the same front door Nicki was so dead set on slamming shut as she'd storm out.

Of course, the Rapture changed everything. Not only did it change Nicki's dramatic exit; it changed the entire world. Things were never to be the same.

After crashing headfirst into the door, it wasn't but a second or two when a rumbling earthquake, mild but very distinct, would rattle the windows and gently

IT WAS A FREEWILL RAPTURE

jostle them about. Just as quick, the darkness was gone and all was still. Two...? Three or four minutes...? It was really hard to say at this point as to how long the miracle lasted.

In its coming and going though; it was enough time to gather all those who've died in the arms of the Lord and His Gospel since the beginning. It was enough time for the angels to gather the innocence; all the children, the unborn, and the mentally blameless. It was enough time for the believers to choose as to whether or not to go. Lastly, and perhaps more importantly, it was enough time for the entire world to absorb a most powerful message noted in the Scriptures.

"So that you may know that I Am God...,"

It would not only seize the world and capture the peoples undivided attention; it would cast them into utter fear, agony, and awe.

Matthew 25:1-2 *"At that time, the kingdom of heaven will be like ten maidens who took their lamps and went out to meet the bridegroom. Five of them were foolish and five were wise."*

Jesus

-Chapter Eight-
REMEMBER LOT'S WIFE

Although a little wobbly and out of breath, Nicki jumped straight to her feet and went into a hysterical fit of bewildered rage. Leah, on the other hand, was more subdued. Every ounce of energy had drained out of her through the fiasco. She had no desire, nor the capacity to tap into Nicki's adrenaline rush. She was sluggish; as if she didn't even want to get up, like a groggy child on a school day. It took a few minutes, but she managed to crawl over to the couch and pull herself up; moaning and groaning the entire way.

She just sat there in a daze; trying to process what had just happened, as was Nicki. Nicki however wasn't in a stupor like her mom. She was on fire. The whole time, even while Leah was struggling to get to the couch, Nicki was going on and on.

IT WAS A FREEWILL RAPTURE

"What the hell…? Oh, my God! What the hell was that, mom? MOM…!" she screamed.

She was just yelling and babbling; cursing every other word. In the heat of the moment, it was clearly more about venting than getting immediate answers. Heavily breathing, yet short on breath, ranting and raving, walking back and forth trying to shake it off and gather her thoughts would take the little seventeen-year-old teenager on a head spinning journey into madness right there in her own living room.

Wound up like a clock, quivering, sneakily peeking out the windows, frantically searching for her phone — Nicki Dawn's helplessness and littleness was quite telling. Turning on the TV and the radio, jumping online, getting through to someone, anyone for that matter, on her phone, on social media; all proved to be futile. Just like Randy, she desperately wanted to get some details as to what was going on. Everybody did — the entire world.

At the moment, they were all getting the same thing; static, mixed signals, and silence. The power grid was shut down — worldwide. Yet, the world had no way of knowing it was a worldwide issue. With all communications mysteriously cut off; how could anyone know. Most, just assumed the shutdowns were local; as did Nicki.

Frustrated, having no luck with outside

DAVID ALAN SMITH

communications, she'd just go back to galivanting around the apartment like a maniacal security guard. She could see and hear people outside of their apartment going crazy. She wasn't however brave enough to get in the mix. Peeking out the window was as far as she'd go.

All sorts of thoughts zipped in and out of her head. Radiation, contagion, disease, alien attack, zombie apocalypse; she just didn't know. And being that she didn't know, she played it safe. With the doors locked, windows shut, and the blinds down, she'd hold up inside; with her mom — at least for the time being.

Leah had also gone off into her own little world of madness. It was where her emotional rollercoaster of sorrow and anger began. The whole time Nicki was carrying on, Leah just sat there on the couch like a vegetable, staring up at the yellowed acoustic ceiling as if she was looking out into space. Nicki tried to engage her; but Leah was totally unresponsive, and Nicki was to revved up to notice.

When Leah truly had to accept what she had just lost, what she had actually missed...; it hit her hard. It hit her..., really, really hard. She slid off the couch and dropped to her knees, right there in the middle of the living room. She then keeled over and rolled into a fetal position only to weep uncontrollably in agony.

It would be Leah who would truly know the

IT WAS A FREEWILL RAPTURE

meaning of being 'left behind'. It wasn't however supposed to be this way. Being left behind wasn't supposed to be for believers.

According to all the books, movies, documentaries and pulpits; the believers were supposed to be instantly and automatically whisked away, right out of their socks, gone in the 'twinkling of an eye', without warning. Sadly, for Leah and so many others, it wasn't quite that simple. Nor was it supposed to be, apparently.

In short, Leah was misled; in a sense, indoctrinated with a false impression. She was led to believe she was ready for the Rapture of the Church when in truth..., she wasn't; as so many others had to find out. They saw a movie and they assumed. They read a book, heard a pastor, watched a documentary; and they assumed.

Led to believe it was all about..., 'POOF...! YOU'RE GONE...' proved to be, not only a misinterpretation of the scriptures, but a costly mistake for many believers; too many for that matter. Unfortunately, Leah was one of the many paying a price.

She lost her chance in a way she never expected. She wasn't prepared. It was as simple as that. She was worthy to be raptured, she was ready to be raptured, but she wasn't prepared.

She never dreamed she'd have to make a decision as to whether or not to go. She had no idea God's gift of freewill would pertain to the Rapture. She wasn't taught this, let alone warned of it. Or was she…?

In his parable, Jesus spoke of 'ten maidens'; five who prepared, and five who didn't. Ten maidens eagerly waiting for the bridegroom's arrival — ten believers; not five believers and five unbelievers. Like the Rapture, his arrival was imminent and sure, but the exact time was hidden from them. So, the anticipating maidens waited, knowing he would come whilst knowing he could come at any moment.

All ten maidens believed he was coming. All ten knew he was coming. It could even be said that all ten maidens were ready; as were all believers in the Rapture. It would however be only five of them who would go. Five left with the bridegroom, because of the ten, only five were truly prepared to address the variants in regards to the bridegroom's arrival.

In all fairness, Jesus' parable has always been subject to mixed interpretations. How could any believer equate their failure to respond to the Rapture to the failure of five maidens not having enough lamp oil to venture into the night to greet the bridegroom. It's a stretch, but the message remains. Being ready, and anticipating cannot fill the shoes of being prepared. They are entirely two different things.

Still, if the parable of the Ten Maidens wasn't enough, perhaps the more direct description of the

IT WAS A FREEWILL RAPTURE

Rapture would have helped the believers know what to prepare for, or possibly expect. Jesus could not have been clearer.

"In that day, he who is on the housetop, and his goods are in the house, let him not come down to take them away. And likewise, the one, who is in the field, let him not turn back. Remember Lot's wife."

How easy and effortless would it have been for Leah to just sit there and instantly disappear like in the movies; or even picked up like a helpless infant and carried away. Right now, she can only wish it did go down that way. But, sadly, it didn't, and now she knows.

She now knows there's nothing about sitting there and instantly disappearing when it comes to being on the rooftop and running back down into the house to gather goods. There's nothing about sitting there and being instantly snatched up like a helpless infant when it comes to being in a field and turning back. And Lot's wife...? Hesitation; to stop, think twice, turn around and look back? How can 'second thoughts' possibly square with 'poof—you're gone'; disappearing or taken in a split-second?

As for Leah, she wasn't on a housetop. Nor was she in a field. She was right there in her living room. Yet, she tarried just the same.

She hesitated, she stopped, turned around, looked

103

back, and went back into the thick of the world. She had to go back and do something first; get something first before she'd go. She was one of the five maidens who first needed to go back and get lamp oil first, and then she'll go with bridegroom.

Had she known, had she thought to ask; since when did the parable of the Ten Maidens depict believers and non-believers? All ten were believers and only half of them went. And since when did…, *'one will be taken and the other left.'*…, pertain to believers and non-believers?

Had she been taught, or at least taken in consideration that one believer will be taken and the other believer left; perhaps she, as well as many others would not have balked and fumbled with the 'freewill rapture' the way they did. Perhaps they would have been a little more prepared for it instead of entertaining the high-flying notion of just sitting there one second and the next second they'd be gone.

It's too late now. It just goes to show that just because something is popular doesn't necessarily make it true. Satan can vouch for that. The movies, the books, the documentaries, and pulpits? Like Peter telling Jesus not to go into Jerusalem, even though their hearts were in the right place and filled to the brim with love and the best of intentions; they proved to take a toll on many believers who weren't ready or

IT WAS A FREEWILL RAPTURE

familiar with the 'freewill rapture'.

The only thing they managed to do was prepare the believers to be unprepared with a false assumption. They won't need extra lamp oil. They won't need to take it upon themselves to go out and greet the bridegroom. The only thing they need to do is believe; just sit there like a bump on a log and believe, and the bridegroom will swoop in and pluck them off the log and carry them away to paradise. If only?

Like Leah, too many believers were caught off guard instead of caught up in the clouds. Too many believers assumed the Rapture was judgment; the righteous go up and the unrighteous don't. The believers go, the unbelievers don't. They were wrong.

The Rapture wasn't judgment, it was just an opportunity. It wasn't so much about Jesus saving His own from the Tribulation to come as it was Jesus giving His own an opportunity to escape it. As it sits; some seized the opportunity…, some didn't. It's end — so many believers; brave, so courageous and confident to think themselves as being one who would be willing to die for Jesus found out that they weren't even able to take His hand and peacefully walk away with Him.

'Zap…, you're gone' would have been nice, and extraordinarily convenient, but being the Rapture didn't go down that way only left believers like Leah broken, and very, very angry.

DAVID ALAN SMITH

Snapping right out of her fetal position. Straightening her posture, rigid and clinching her fist in rage, Leah again found herself looking straight up at the ceiling, yelling at the top of her lungs with everything she had.

"IT...ISN'T...FAIR...!" she screamed.

Sharp, loud, and to the point. She so wanted to blame God, blame Jesus for her own lack of better judgment. But then again, was it bad judgment to stay? Like vocal cannonballs, she'd fire them off one by one; scolding God, scolding Jesus. She had to let them know that it was their fault, not hers as to why she lost her chance.

"WHY...? WHY...?" she blasted. "You know I wanted to go. You know I would have gone. You should have waited, if you had only waited? I believed you! I trusted you!"

She gasped and took in another big breath and shouted again, even louder.

"WHY COULDN'T YOU HAVE WAITED? Is this how you treat those who love you? Is this how you repay all those who have given their life to you? And trusted you? You leave us here to...DIE! Or expect us to just take off and leave our children behind to DIE! This isn't the way it was supposed to be! DAMN IT!!!" She yelled.

It went on and on. Back and forth; bawling in

IT WAS A FREEWILL RAPTURE

agony one minute and livid the next. Nicki would have to step back every time Leah would be charged to vent her anger. Wisely, she dared not speak a word to her at the height of her fury. No words of comfort, no words of encouragement or agreement…, nothing. She remained silent and still.

Nicki wasn't about to leave her though. She would patiently wait it out. She'd go back to peeking out the windows, checking the TV, attempt to make some calls, but she'd be more than ready to approach her mother after each and every fit of rage.

After the fury would subside, again and again Nicki would not hesitate to tenderly slide in next to her and absorb as much tension and pain as she possibly could. It would be then and only then, after Leah had simmered down that Nicki dared to utter a word to her mother. Even then, there wasn't much to say. Still, though the words were short and few, they were meaningful and straight from the heart.

"I'm sorry, mom. I'm so sorry," was about all Nicki could find in herself to say.

She couldn't help but feel guilty. After listening to her mother's raving rants and prayers come and go, she pretty much got it. Nicki understood why her mom was so upset in a way that totally differed from the reason why she was upset. Nicki was flat out frightened and scared; Leah on the other hand was

DAVID ALAN SMITH

suffering a broken heart.

Nicki knew the whole concept of the Rapture of the Church, being that her mom and Joel shared it with her over the years. Scoffing and rolling her eyes this time however was no longer an option. Even though Nicki really couldn't bring herself to say for sure it was the Rapture and her mom actually missed it; whether it was or wasn't, her mom thought it so. It would only go on to say her mom actually missed her chance to be raptured because of her.

Leah came back for her. Nicki knows this. And this is why she's touched with a sense of guilt. This is why she was more inclined to say sorry to her grief-stricken mother more than anything else.

Sitting on the floor, in the corner up against the living room wall, the loving daughter cradled her mom in her arms. Rocking back and forth, Leah's face buried on the side of Nicki's neck, she'd weep irrepressibly. It's been about an hour now, more or less; and this is about the third time Nicki has moved in to console her.

It truly was breaking her heart to see her mom so broken. It took her right back to her childhood. She remembered how it broke her heart back then. And like then, she would cry with her mother.

Whimpering, "Mom…, mom please…," she softly whispered. But it wasn't the only whisper in the room.

IT WAS A FREEWILL RAPTURE

Out of nowhere, a name; "Dmitri…," slithered into Nicki's ear.

It startled her. She heard it. She heard it quite clearly and instantly recoiled with a quick turn of her head.

Still holding her mother, she tensed up. She cocked her neck to look at her mother, so as to see if she had heard it too, but Leah didn't hear it. She was still quite occupied with her sorrow. Nicki had to ask herself if she really heard it. She was sure it wasn't a voice in her head. It was a voice by her head, it whispered right into her ear; a low raspy whisper.

"Dmitri…," she uttered aloud so as to confirm what she thought she heard.

"What the hell…?" she murmured so as to question it.

It took a few minutes to adjust and halfway pretend she didn't actually hear the voice or anything at all for that matter. She reluctantly shrugged it off and melted back into comforting her mom.

She didn't know Dmitri was in the room. How could she? Dmitri was a demon-angel; an Influencer—unseen, but very present.

He had a job to do.

1 Peter 5:8 *'Be sober; be vigilant; because your adversary the devil walks about like a roaring lion, seeking whom he may devour.'*

-Chapter Nine-
DEMONS DELIGHT

Nicki Dawn, this day, was now on the menu. And Dmitri was there to prepare and eventually serve her soul to the devil; of whom he will devour if she isn't careful.

Dmitri would be just one of uncountable others liberated and free to do what they hadn't been able to do up unto the Rapture; of which they, the demons, refer to as the 'Nazarene's Harvest'. Foretold in the Bible, *'the hand'* was lifted with the Raptures' coming and going—which is to say the Holy Spirit of God has been removed.

In turn, as promised in so many words; all the demons devious desires that had been faithfully kept in check and down to a bare minimal by the Holy Spirit were now unleashed—free to do what they've longed to do. And they weren't wasting any time. Here, it hadn't even been but a little over an hour since the

IT WAS A FREEWILL RAPTURE

Rapture, and the demons were already at it with fervor.

At the moment, Dmitri was delighted. It would be the first time he would actually hear one of them; one of the created children refer to him by name. Even though he found it to be so delightful to hear his name spoken aloud, he knew it wasn't time for fun and games. Being an Influencer, a superior kind of demon, equivalent to 'special forces' in the military, Dmitri was well disciplined. He's on a mission, and he's not about to screw it up with cheap tricks.

As always; patience, stealth, and timing would lead to perfection. The watchful demon would wait. He'd wait for Nicki to unknowingly open a window into her mind so as to let him slither in and do what he's been ordered to do; lure her away from 'the truth, the whole truth, and nothing but the truth'. He's there to deceive her, and manipulate her; as the *powers of darkness* are called to do; and do so well.

A good fifteen minutes or so had passed since Nicki uttered Dmitri's name. In that time, Leah went numb again. No yelling, no crying, just blankly staring at the wall in front of her as her head lay in Nicki's lap. Caressing her mother's face and hair ever so gently, Nicki drifted off into the land of thinking about things.

Even though she could hear the commotion still brewing outside; she ignored it long enough to make

DAVID ALAN SMITH

an attempt to sort things out. She found herself quietly dissecting everything that went down. It only led her to reflect on what her mom and Joel had told her about the Rapture, Jesus and God and the Gospel and all that other Bible stuff that she always referred to as crap and nonsense.

Leah jolted ever so slightly, as if she was dodging something in a dream, but it wasn't enough to break her hypnotic stare. It did however shift Nicki's direction of thought. She again focused on how her mom fell to such heart wrenching depths and why. In turn, she'd only find herself once again laden with a burning guilt.

If it really was the Rapture, the whole idea of being taken into heaven, and to think her mom gave it up for her—her miserable, rude and hateful daughter; it weighed heavy on Nicki's heart. She couldn't help but blame herself for her mom's anguish. She took in a deep breath and let out another loaded sigh. Despite her mom being totally out of it and unresponsive, Nicki felt the urge to speak to her yet again.

Already welling up in tears, she'd let it out; her innermost feelings. She'd let her mother know her sentiments.

"Ah…, mom, I'm so sorry mom. I'm sorry, I'm sorry…, I'm sorry," she said ever so gently, but firm just the same.

IT WAS A FREEWILL RAPTURE

Within a couple of seconds something else would unexpectedly roll out of Nicki's mouth. "Oh, God..., GOD, I'm so sorry."

Involuntarily setting her sights on God, even for just a moment, there would be hope for what was once a godless Nicki. Her mention of God was ever so quick, but it was a start. Dmitri cringed and jeered. This is the exact thing he needs to crush; and he'd do it with pleasure.

Pouring her heart out, "Mom..., mom," she sobbed. "I'm so sorry..., please forgive me."

The repetitive heart wrenching plea would send Nicki crashing into an emotional breakdown. Eye's tightly clinched shut, dropping her head into her chest, taking it all in for a few seconds, only to erupt with a burst of tears like an overdue volcano is what came out of Nicki's soul this time when she apologized. It would however be the open window Dmitri would be looking for. And he didn't hesitate to sneak in like a ninja-burglar slipping into a home.

As much as he wanted to whisper loud enough as he did when he spoke his name into her ear, or physically hurt her like the 'crossover demons', he wouldn't. There'd be plenty enough time for that in due course. As of now, his stealth mattered most.

He did not want to scare the fish away. Besides, he'd do well to follow orders. Lucifer had plans, big plans and there would be no room for personal agendas or insubordination. With that said, Dmitri would go back to the basics; tactics used to lure the fish, not scare them away. He'd take his powers of communicating back down and whisper just loud enough into Nicki's ear to deliver…thoughts…, not words.

As soon as Nicki caught her breath and regained her composure, the scheming demon-angel snuggled in close, real close — almost cuddling.

"Why are you saying sorry," he delicately whispered. "She was ready to leave you. In fact, she wanted to leave. She was hoping to leave you. And…you're… saying sorry…to her?"

The hook was beautifully place, and the bait was tantalizing. It caught Nicki's attention. Dmitri however was far from finished.

"Oh yeah, yeah…, sure…, she came back for you, but look at how pissed off she is that she did. She's crying her eyes out…? You call that love? She's hating it — hating that she's still here — stuck with you. And look at you…?" Dmitri hissed to shame her. "Sitting there coddling her, and comforting her when you know damn well, she despises the thought of being here with you — all pissed off that she lost her chance to leave you."

The scheming demon reasoned ever so subtly. He was shrewd to perfection. The crafty persuasion

IT WAS A FREEWILL RAPTURE

went on; not too much and not too fast. Prodding and kneading Nicki's mind; stirring up emotions and doubts. He'd poke her with one piercing thought after another; sticking them into head like pinpoints and tacks.

It eventually worked like a charm. Nicki digested Dmitri's articulate and sinister whispers like spoon fed applesauce. It went down smooth. She weighed them out, and it wasn't to Leah's favor. Nicki's heart actually started to gloss over. She'd look off and jeer at the thoughts. It wasn't enough for her to glare at her grieving mom, but it surely broke any kind of deeper affection she had for her.

She stopped caressing her hair, loosened her hold, and started to sneakily scoot out from underneath Leah's resting head, when — BAM..., BAM..., BAM..., echoed through the apartment. It jolted Nicki; it was so loud.

It was a frantic knock, someone pounding on the door. It also yanked Leah out of her stupor. They both instantly tensed up. With all the sirens and commotion going on, they didn't know what to expect. Faction Eight Enforcers, DSS, neighbors, Joel, friends, they just didn't know.

BAM..., BAM, "Nicki..., Nicki..., are you in there?"

Nicki quickly, but cautiously made her way across the living room. She didn't go straight for the door

∽ 115 ∽

DAVID ALAN SMITH

though. She would instead maneuver off to the side. Bent down, she slowly crept over to the near window, barely tweaked the two bottom blinds and carefully squeaked a peak outside.

She was pretty sure she already knew who it was. The voice, a voice she knows well, pretty much gave it away. Still, she wasn't going to take any chances.

Bang…, bang, bang, bang…again came blasting and echoing through the room.

"Nicki…? Nicki…?" the voice outside the door shouted, impatiently and now a bit irritated.

Just as Nicki thought, peeking through the blinds, it was Chad, her boyfriend. He was alone. She hurried to the door, unlocked it to let him in. Chad just barged in even before the door was completely open. Nicki quickly locked the door behind him after scolding him to get the heck out of the way. In a panic, like everyone else he too would start his rant.

"Nicki…," he panted, "are you ok? Man…, I'm so glad you're here. People…, a lot of people and children have been snatched by aliens or something. They're gone, flat out gone. My neighbors' kids gone and other people, I…I can't even keep track…, and…, and-"

"Chad, Chad, Chad…, take it easy. Calm down," Nicki ordered. "Just take it easy, slow down."

"They weren't taken by aliens," Leah interrupted with a somber and defeated tone.

∽ 116 ∽

IT WAS A FREEWILL RAPTURE

"What…!" Chad barked as he curled up his lip and jeered at her.

"Never mind her right now," Nicki asserted. "What do you know? What's happening out there? I mean our TV, the radio and the internet, our cell phones…, nothings working."

Gulping and panting…, "Yeah, I know. I tried to call you right away, but couldn't get through," he said. "I couldn't move, Nicki. Nobody could move. Danny and Juan…, we couldn't move. Everybody, the cars, and the people everything just stopped." He practically yelled.

"I know, I know," Nicki shared, "I couldn't move either. But cars…, and stuff — what do you mean?"

"Yeah…, cars, buses, everything froze — dogs, birds in the air…, everything!" he clamored. "And all of these little light thingies', like glowing balls, orbs — they were like swimming around and whisking past people and… and in and out of cars and buildings, going right through the walls. They were taking the kids, the little kids." he shouted as he ran out of breath.

Nicki just stood there, dumbfounded. "The kids…?" she retorted.

"Yeah…, the kids, young children — they were frickin' being abducted by those balls of light. I saw a couple of kids, too — all excited and giggling, run into, like…, like, I don't know — this glowing doorway

∞ 117 ∞

DAVID ALAN SMITH

thing too. They ran straight into it like it was a ride at Disneyland. And…, they disappeared. And their moms…?" he groaned.

"OMG…, they were just screaming out of their minds. Cuz they couldn't frickin' move—either could I. Nobody could move or…or do anything. We couldn't run, we couldn't fight them, or chase after them, we just had to sit there and watch. It was crazy!" He clamored.

Nicki tried to respond, but all she did was stutter. She just couldn't quite grasp all that Chad was saying; and saying so fast. Before she could get anything legible out of her mouth, Chad immediately jumped back in.

Getting sappy, and laying it on thick, "I'm scared out of my mind, babe. I was so worried—I'm so glad you're ok. Here…," He whimpered as he inched in close to hug her.

Nicki just shunned him though; scoffed and pushed him away. She's a tough girl; independent, you might say. She's never been the needy 'hold me tight' type. Besides, she was never really into Chad. Their relationship, at least from her perspective, was more about image, or convenience than sentimental. There was no love, no affection; at least coming from her side of the fence.

Still, Chad's hysterical update was a lot to process.

IT WAS A FREEWILL RAPTURE

Piling all that on top of her own heap of troubles didn't help. Speechless, Nicki just flopped and sunk down into the couch. She'd run her hands over her face and plant them in front of her mouth, held together like praying.

She looked over to Leah, "Mom...?" she said, in a tone seeking her opinion, or some sort of guidance.

Still sitting on the floor with her back against the wall, Leah just gazed at her and slowly shook her head. She was still half delirious, but sober enough to know there was really nothing they could do. She heard everything that Chad had to say. It was incredible to say the least.

"Wait," she muttered. "We just have to wait, Nicki. The TV, the radio..., phones? They'll kick back on. We'll know soon enough what to do or...," she paused, "or what not to do."

Just then; a sound, a good sound slipped into the room. Soft, precious; it was sweet. And beckoning.

"Mew—"

"Oh my God...," Nicki blurted, as she sprang up off the couch.

It was Sheefoo. It was their cat, a little yellow and orange tabby. Nicki brought her home as a tiny little four-week-old kitten years ago promising to take care of her. Of course, it was Leah who'd end up being the caretaker. Still, it was their precious little kitty, their

∞ 119 ∞

little friend barely peeking past the bedroom door, frightened and leery.

She's been hiding under the bed this whole time. Her sweet innocent little high-pitched meow, even though it was a frightened meow, it was enough to remind Leah and Nicki all was not lost. It was a joy, even a blessing to hear Sheefoo. The tension in the room instantly went down a notch.

"C'mon baby," Nicki would say as she beckoned her with her hand. "C'mon, baby—it's ok."

Sheefoo was too scared. Everything going on, Chad there didn't help. The little kitty was always timid and cautious around other people, more so males. Leah and Nicki were the only two she felt comfortable with. She wasn't a total recluse though. She'd eventually warm up to others, but it was always slow and careful. Joel even had a hard time getting close to the precious little feline, but they eventually bonded.

"Come here…, Sheefoo…, its ok girl. C'mon…," Nicki urged as soft and gentle as she could. Knowing she wasn't going to budge, clearly too scared, Nicki scooted right up to her. She tenderly picked her little baby up into her arms and went back to the couch, consoling her.

Chad, still nerve-stricken, but not enough to keep him from getting a little jealous would slightly sneer at the cat clearly getting more attention than him. He

IT WAS A FREEWILL RAPTURE

again tried to slide in close to Nicki so as to get into the mix with all the affection. While sneakily wrapping his arm around her he reached over to pet Sheefoo sitting on Nicki's lap, but Sheefoo too would shun him. She hissed and took a swipe at him. Chad quickly jerked away.

"Frickin' little....," he snapped.

Nicki was shocked, not at Chad, but at Sheefoo. She's never ever done that, to anyone ever. Nicki didn't know what to think. She just went back to coddle and pet Sheefoo that much more; giving her the benefit of the doubt.

"She's probably scared with everything going on. I mean look at us? Look how freaked out we are." she reasoned.

Leah just looked on. She had a sneaky suspicion there was more to Sheefoo's behavior than just being scared. There was something wrong, she could just feel it. She didn't know how right she was. Dmitri was still there. He never left. He's been there all along; watching and listening to them carrying on.

He loathed them so; Nicki, Chad, but mostly Leah, she was of the Nazarene. It was because of her; he was assigned to Nicki. He's there to sabotage any influence Leah may have on her daughter. If there's to be any influence, it would be from him, the Influencer; there to keep Nicki in darkness—away from the light of the

DAVID ALAN SMITH

truth; as far away from the Nazarene as possible.

Those of the Nazarene, like Leah, were protected by guardian angels, but those close to them; not so much. Still, they had an edge. Those like Nicki Dawn; who had even the slightest chance to be swayed by those of the Nazarene, needed to be kept at bay. Any gravitating towards the light, would need to be thwarted at all cost. And Dmitri was there to make sure Nicki didn't do such a thing as that.

Standing in the midst, the cat caught Dmitri's attention. He was already informed the animals would be used extensively after the Nazarene's Harvest; as part of Lucifer's master plan. With the hand of the Holy Spirit removed; such things are now possible for them. Not since the days of Noah has such liberty been granted to them. And they will take their liberties to the hilt.

From this day forward it'll be all about the *'signs and wonders'* spoken of in the Bible; referring to the powers of Satan unleashed on mankind. And the animals would have a part in these *signs and wonders.* Right now, they're merely being used to set the stage. The show itself — the darkest show of all time — will premiere in due course.

Feigning affection, "Ahh…, now isn't that sweet." Dmitri praised as Nicki continued to console Sheefoo with her kitty-talk.

IT WAS A FREEWILL RAPTURE

There, by his side, was another demon that he had summoned. It was one of his subordinate angels from the ranks of *'legion'*, lower end demons — the expendable ones. Knowing he's now free to do so, Dmitri ordered his lesser to enter the cat, possess it, and control it to do their bidding. The dutiful demon of *'legion'* was prompt. Without a fuss, without question, and with the greatest of ease; into the cat he'd go.

In seconds, Sheefoo started trembling, nearly convulsing. "What's wrong, sweetie," Nicki pressed, "it's alright…, its ok, baby."

She drew her face down close to Sheefoo to snuggle noses, but a sweet little snuggle wasn't in the stars. Sheefoo hissed again, viciously. Nicki jerked back along with an attempt to push the cat off her lap, but just as quick, the cat made its move. Sheefoo, no longer being Sheefoo, lunged at Chad. It was straight for his face.

Chad screamed as he rolled over the back of the couch. The cat tore into Chad as ferociously as it could. As fast as Chad would grab the cat to toss it aside it would attack again just as fast. His eyes, being immediately injured by the cats' claws were clinched shut and bleeding. He couldn't see.

Screaming bloody murder, he'd crawl, roll and struggle to get back on his feet only to trip and bump into things and fall back down. The cat scratching and

∞ 123 ∞

DAVID ALAN SMITH

biting was merciless. Leah and Nicki didn't linger they were on top of it just as quick as it happened. Yelling as well, they were there helping Chad, trying to push, grab and even kick the cat off of him.

In the other dimension, Dmitri was laughing. He loved it. He was getting quite the show. The *'legion'* demon was tearing it up, but was eventually hit and pounded on enough to be chased away. It took a run around the living room and secured itself under a little end table.

With its claws dug into the carpet, hissing, and glaring; the demon-possessed cat clearly wasn't finished with its attack. Its eyes..., the eyes weren't the eyes of Sheefoo. They were, but they weren't. They were eerily reddish; like redeye captured in photographs. Her fur standing on end made it even more ominous.

Chad, by this time was squirming and crying in pain. He was torn up. His face, his eyes, his neck, arms, his back, even his legs were ripped up, scratched up and bleeding. The cat's claws and teeth slashed right through his clothes like razors. Cussing and bawling, Chad was now getting plenty of attention.

Both Leah and Nicki were tending to him and his wounds the best they could. They would however do so without taking their eyes off Sheefoo; no more than a couple of seconds at a time. Nicki would quickly grab

∞ 124 ∞

IT WAS A FREEWILL RAPTURE

her cell phone and call 911. She figured she wouldn't get any response, but she thought she'd try. Getting zero response, she tossed it down as fast as she picked it up.

"I'm going to get some towels and bandages," Leah clamored as she scampered off to the bathroom.

It wasn't but a minute before round two would ensue. While Leah was down the hall, Dmitri would ring the bell if you will. He'd sound off another order summoning his underling to attack again.

Unhesitant, the cat, in stalking mode would slink and slither a couple of steps before it would jet across the floor and catapult itself off of the couch. It flew right across the room like a rocket. Nicki, catching the flying leap in the corner of her eye, by impulse turned and ducked. Chad would not be so fortunate.

The cat was back on him trying to kill him, if it could. This time survival instincts kicked in. Within seconds, Chad grabbed the cat already tearing into his shoulder. With everything he had, with his hands wrapped around the cat's neck, he rolled over on top of it and—"snap"! He snapped Sheefoo's neck and threw her across the room.

"F...!" he yelled, "F—ing thing...!"

Dmitri was still laughing uncontrollably. His subordinate was gone, lost to the *imprisonment of outer darkness*, but it was worth it. Besides, it's what the

∽ 125 ∽

DAVID ALAN SMITH

'legion' demons do. They're expendable, they're plentiful, but more importantly they're devoted. Their sacrificial loyalty to serve Satan was determined long ago, even before the rebellion in heaven. Being their numbers are uncountable, like sand on the beach, they've proven to be quite useful. As just seen.

After the tense battle and seeing her cherished Sheefoo lifeless on the floor, Nicki started to bawl. By this time, Leah was back with the towels and first-aid. She heard the short-lived commotion and was out in seconds. She too saw Sheefoo lying dead on the floor.

"Oh, no…, oh God…, Lord no…," she moaned in anguish.

Chad was miserably groaning and whimpering. Nicki was split, she was torn. She wanted to care for Sheefoo, but Chad was the one clearly in need of attention. She was hysterically sobbing and shaking.

Handing Nicki one of the towels she had brought out, "Go, see if she's ok," Leah said as she started to address Chad's wounds.

Nicki crawled over to her little baby. She was still afraid of her. Trembling, she'd slowly reach down to wrap the towel over and around her lifeless little kitty. For no reason other than caution, she'd pull back a bit, but go at it again.

It wasn't but moments before she had Sheefoo wrapped up and holding her close to her bosom. Nicki

126

IT WAS A FREEWILL RAPTURE

couldn't help but burst in tears like a dam giving way as she held her loving pet as close to her as she possibly could. She cradled and rocked with sorrow…, so much sorrow.

Sorrow…? It was everywhere; as was uncertainty and unthinkable fear. All three emotions had mercilessly imprisoned the entire planet; gripped it by the throat and choking the life out of it. And it hadn't even been but two hours into the nightmare.

Revelation 13:18 *"Here is wisdom. Let him who has understanding calculate the number of the beast…, for it is the number of a man: His number is 666."*

❦

-Chapter Ten-

'…666…'

U p north, Randy finally made it back home. It was a trip from hell. What would have taken him forty-five minutes at most any other day took him well over ten hours. It was because the entire trip was flooded with similar things he encountered back where Joel disappeared.

Vanishings, countless accidents, animal attacks, stormy weather, on top of plane wrecks and mobs going crazy in Carson City…, there was just too much to take in. Inching his way back, bumper to bumper, with no radio or phone really took him over the edge. It in fact drove him crazy, enough to where he mentally lost it a couple of times. Even so, thankfully, he'd manage to regain his composure each time, but it wasn't easy.

The only thing that saved him was the radio. It did eventually kick on towards the end, for a couple

IT WAS A FREEWILL RAPTURE

hours. It was just an Emergency Broadcasting System loop, but it was better than nothing. He heard it so many times that he's pretty much memorized it.

From it, he was at least able to get a snapshot as to what was going on and how extensive the crisis was. Over and over, loop after loop; a dry, mundane, almost robotic feminine voice spilled the beans.

"This is the Emergency Broadcast System. To repeat, the entire world is in a state of emergency. We are now getting confirmed reports that the mysterious attack and ensuing storms appear to be worldwide. Europe, China, Russia, the Middle East, Africa..., all continents are experiencing and reporting the same as is the United STATE of America.

In like manner, the temporary, but inexplicable, holding and restraints on all aspects of life; people and transportation were simultaneous and global in nature. The vanishings, as well, is an international affair. An undisclosed number of people have vanished, but it is being reported that the children, particularly younger children and infants were targeted. Ages, common factors, common threads have not yet been determined.

Also, the sudden surge of animal attacks, both wild and domestic animals continue to spread and worsen. Injuries and fatalities resulting from the attacks increasingly persist. Global citizens are to take

DAVID ALAN SMITH

extra precautions to avoid and avert any and all contact with all animals and their pets.

Pet owners need to isolate or quarantine their pets until further notice. It has not yet been determined as to whether or not the animals are rabid, infected, suffering from dementia, or contagious. As to how and why the animals are affected by the international assault is still unknown and under investigation.

All hospitals, clinics, emergency rooms, medical facilities and enforcer departments are inundated, understaffed and operating beyond sustainable capacity. Citizens, if at all possible, are strongly advised not to burden their operating procedures outside of extreme and/or life-threatening situations and injuries until further notice. All citizens are strongly advised to seek refuge and remain indoors until further developments.

President Manning via Vice President Hill has declared Martial Law. Military Units are being dispatched and deployed in various regions to establish order. Above all…, remain calm. Panic as of now is our worst enemy. Please remain calm. This is the Emergency Broadcasting Network. To repeat, the entire world is in a state of emergency."

And on and on it went. Hearing it so many times, over and over, was almost torture in itself. Still, the briefing helped, and Randy was more than thankful it came on when it did.

IT WAS A FREEWILL RAPTURE

When he got back into Tahoe, having gone straight to Jake and Becky's house, Randy discovered things were far worse there than they were at the scene of the accident—where Joel disappeared. Inside the three-bedroom house quietly planted in a carpet of pine trees just outside the city limits; the three found themselves frantically searching for some answers—just like the people were at the scene of the accident.

Rebecca was, by far, the most unraveled; at par with the lady carrying on about her missing daughter is how Randy saw it. She was broken, completely broken.

Pursuit of the truth, for them and the rest of the world, even hours on in, was just beginning. Sitting in a dark house with no electricity didn't help. Why the power was still off at Jake and Rebecca's home was yet another question, but it paled to the bigger questions screaming for answers.

Being lit with candles and flashlights, the living room was dim. In it, Becky's hands nervously trembled as she clumsily raced and thumbed through the pages of her brothers Bible. Frantic, with her eye's swollen red and crying, she just had to find the scripture that Joel was talking about in the letter they had just found in the bindings of his Bible.

Jake, her husband of thirteen years and Randy, both who were just as nerve-stricken as she was, anxiously

∞ 131 ∞

DAVID ALAN SMITH

loomed and peered over her shoulder as she sat at the desk recklessly flipping through the pages of the Bible in search of 2 Thessalonians.

In their minds, there was absolutely no time to waste. Every moment seemed to count. Understandably, time seemed to be of the essence in light of what was going on and what happened just past daybreak.

"Here, Becky...., give it to me", Randy softly ordered and gently slid the Bible from Rebecca's shaking hands. He could see she was totally disoriented, lost and unable to focus.

Leaving Rebecca at the desk and maneuvering to the nearby kitchen table as he peered through the 'book of ages' more rationally, he sat down and within seconds, thumbed his way through the pages and found 2 Thessalonians neatly tucked away in the same exact place as it had been for centuries. Jake closely followed Randy as if he was tied to him, holding and shining a flashlight over Randy's shoulders so he would be better able to see and read.

"Second Thessalonians, chapter two, verse... uh...," Randy stuttered.

Quickly interrupting..., "Verse three to twelve." Jake blurted out as he again glanced at the letter to reaffirm himself.

It was a letter written by Joel. Actually, it was more like a list of scriptures he wanted them to have for a

IT WAS A FREEWILL RAPTURE

time such as this. Randy had totally forgotten about Joel emphatically telling him about the Bible in his suitcase; that there was something there for him. It faded from his memory rather quickly with everything going on.

After remembering it though, they immediately found the letter and started to go over the particular scriptures. The first two on the list didn't help at all. Now on the third one, getting more frantic by the minute; they could only hope this scripture would at least shed a little light on what was going on.

"Read it", Becky anxiously demanded.

"Ok, ok…, let's see"! Randy said.

He quickly slid his finger down the page to the second chapter and the particular scriptures that seemed to be nothing short of treasure. Zeroing in on it, Randy methodically and clearly read them out loud so as to share them with Rebecca and Jake.

"Ok…, this is what it says:

Let no one deceive you by any means; for that Day will not come unless the falling away comes first, and the man of sin is revealed, the son of perdition, who opposes and exalts himself that he is God. Do you not remember that when I was still with you, I told you these things? And now you know what is restraining, that he may be revealed in his own time."

Randy continued…, as both his sister and

DAVID ALAN SMITH

brother-in-law intently listened. *"For the mystery of lawlessness is already at work; only…HE…who now restrains will do so until…HE…is taken out of the way. And then the lawless one will be revealed whom the Lord will consume with the breath of His mouth and destroy with the brightness of His coming. The coming of the lawless one is according to the working of Satan"*.

Randy paused a moment, and slowly repeated the last sentence with a questioning tone, like that of a bewildered and inquisitive detective emphasizing an important piece to a riddled crime; a mysterious clue.

"The coming of the lawless one is according to the working of Satan?" He uttered as he gazed and pondered on the scriptures haunting persona.

Irritable and flirting with hysteria, "What does Satan have to do with all this shit?" Becky screamed as if the scripture was ridiculously stupid and meaningless.

Patience was nowhere to be found in her and for good reason. Randy wasn't about to press it. He quickly went on to finish what he started.

"The coming of the lawless one is according to the working of Satan, with all power, signs, and lying wonders and with all unrighteous deception among those who perish, because they did not receive the love of the truth, that they might be saved".

Slowing the pace, he went on to finish. *"And for*

IT WAS A FREEWILL RAPTURE

this reason, God will send them...strong delusion...that they should...believe...the lie; that they all may be condemned who did not believe the truth, but had...pleasure... in unrighteousness."

"Pleasure in unrighteousness...?" Jake barked and hissed. "What the hell is that supposed to mean? Frickin' Joel — same ol' shit! Him and his Bible crap."

Becky had the same sentiments. Even more irritated, she launched a heated tirade; voicing her own disappointment in the so-called treasure in the Bible.

Sobbing with fury, "What is he talking about...? Believe what lie? Does all this look like a f...ing lie?" she hysterically yelled only to scream even louder. "Where's my baby? I want my babies back. Where are they...? I want them back...! I want them back! I want them back!" she repeated on a downward spiral.

Getting weaker with each word, she faded out like a tool, or a toy with dying batteries winding down to its last breath. Before they knew it, she was back in the fetal position; weeping profusely in Skye's 'Little Mermaid' blanket. Jake moseyed in to comfort her. Randy too just shut down as he dropped into a tailspin of doubts and questions.

Becky didn't know it, neither did Jake and Randy, but she was actually speaking for the entire world. At par with a desperate, strung-out heroin addict crying out; in need of a fix, she needed fast and easy answers.

∞ 135 ∞

DAVID ALAN SMITH

She needed to know what was going on and she needed it now…, right now — like everyone else.

It's now been well over twelve hours into the nightmare. Trying to cope with all that's happened; trying to understand it and make sense of it by searching for quick easy answers with limited resources was proving to be way too much for anyone to handle. It was tormenting and traumatic to even try. But what else are they to do? No telecommunication, no outside reporting or social media left many feeling isolated and helpless; bordering on insanity.

Even though the Bible that lay in the palm of her hands not more than ten minutes ago had its share of answers; it wasn't what Becky wanted, let alone what she needed. The Rapture, no doubt, was bandied about. Randy even brought it up, but it wasn't good enough or solid enough because it didn't bring any comfort or closure.

Like the rest of the world, with Bible in hand, Becky had a good part of the answers she needed, but they are worthless in the hearts of those who feed on what they want; not on what they need. It's the way of the world. The way it's been since the beginning of time; since the Garden of Eden.

Right now, Becky's appetite for what she wants has gone way, way beyond a casual whim or desire. It's now a maniacal craving; a feverish yen. She, Jake,

IT WAS A FREEWILL RAPTURE

everyone is desperate; salivating for some immediate answers. But the answers they seek are not so easily found, because they don't exist outside of the Bible — but then again, maybe they do.

In a world where wishful thinking, lies and half-truths serve as answers..., then yes..., the answers Becky and the rest of the world are clamoring for will once again thrive. They'll be gently laid in the palm of their hands like baby rabbits for them to fondle, caress, and protect from anything that may harm them. Satan plans on it. He's counting on it. He's in fact already started.

Could anything less be expected from whom the Bible calls *'the god of this age'*...? The devil has long anticipated this day; the 'Nazarenes Harvest'. He didn't know when the day would come. Nobody did, not even Jesus, himself — only the Father knew. This however doesn't go on to say he didn't have his plan of attack already in order when the hour came.

Satan's army of demons, numberless at that, knew the drill when the day came. They were ready and prepared. Like grade school children trained with fire drills and mock school-shootings; the demons knew exactly what to do, where to go, and how to go about it at the drop of a hat. They've gone over it plenty of times; more so this generation than any other. It was because Satan had a clue this would be the generation of the Nazarene's Harvest.

He didn't know the hour, but he knew the time frame. '666' was more than enough to tell him the Nazarene's Harvest was imminent. '666'…, *'the number of a man'* wasn't hard for Satan to figure out being he knew the numbers referred to genealogical time. He's the 666th.

Thus, the world's unholy messiah was ordained the day he was born; of whom the…*powers of darkness*…rejoiced, likened to the birth of Christ. Though unaware of it, he's already been groomed, positioned and ready to hit the world stage; just like the *'false prophet'* — who's already secured his authenticity and identity decades ago. He needs only to reemerge.

As he's done with the *'false prophet'*, Satan will orchestrate the grand appearance of whom he's already labeled the 'Universal Christ'. He'll make sure the name sticks and the world receives him as such. He'll know exactly the right time to bring his Christ into the scene of chaos and despair. He'll set it up so as to give the world every reason on earth to deem him the 'Savior'. All in due time, though — all in due time.

First, the stage must be set. With the hand of the Holy Spirit now removed, along with the Church; setting the stage will be a cinch. With his five, most powerful and devoted high-ranking demon-Archangels under his wings; each of them immensely capable,

IT WAS A FREEWILL RAPTURE

empowered, and now positioned and free to capitalize on the Lord's Rapture, Satan will give all the answers the humankind could ever want and hope for.

He who's vowed, '*I shall be like… GOD…; the Most-High*', will have his day to feign his seat on the throne; secure it, if at all possible. Ultimately, if all goes according to his darkest of schemes; the people will revere him as such; as GOD, by name no less. With his '*false prophet*' already in place, and his artificial Holy Spirit and the Antichrist lurking just over the horizon; the Unholy Trinity will be complete.

The only thing he needs to do is woo the people to embrace it; all of them if he had his way. But, not all will. There will be those who will be reluctant to bend a knee to the unholy trinity; even those who will adamantly refuse to do such a thing. How many is yet to be known.

What is known however; Satan in all his prowess, has an extreme advantage. He knows the humankind well; not as well as Jehovah God, but enough to know how vulnerable and predictable they are. Being no different than a dog returning to its vomit, he knows the people will go right back to chasing the things that tickle the ear. Wishful thinking, lies, and half-truths; anything but the whole truth will once again rise to the occasion; and to his advantage.

"*Always learning…, but never able to come to the*

∽ 139 ∽

DAVID ALAN SMITH

knowledge of the truth...," as the Apostle Paul so eloquently puts it; will once again be the clear and present danger. As it sits, the people of the world suffering intolerable torment and despair will be easy to fleece. Becky, in her unraveling hysteria, could easily be the perfect example of just how effortlessly it will be to lure her into darkness.

And dark it is at the moment. Randy quietly sitting across the room gazed at Jake doing all he could to console his sister. She was so broken. Who could blame her; Jake too for that matter? Randy certainly didn't blame them. His heart went out to them.

Their seven-year-old son Sean and Skye, their precious little daughter of only four years old were stolen is the way they saw it. It was however only part of the sorrow and misery that has stabbed them in the heart like a dagger. For not only were their two precious children taken, but their baby, seven months into Becky's pregnancy was also suddenly gone.

Like a vapor, another boy, who they had already come to name Michael Ray, simply seized to exist. As far as they were concerned, their babies were kidnapped; abducted — not saved by way of sparing them from the coming hell on earth, as Randy hinted when he mentioned the Rapture. It didn't go over well at all.

It's why they were finding the few scriptures they read from Joel's list to be so worthless and infuriating.

∽ 140 ∽

IT WAS A FREEWILL RAPTURE

Randy couldn't blame them for that either. Pain and suffering were in control. Fear, uncertainty, and a hailstorm of unanswered questions were the only things left in the air to breath. The only thing they really had to go on is Joel was the one who vanished with the kids—not them.

Deep down, the three of them couldn't help but feel it truly is the Rapture of the Church they're dealing with. But, give it a little time. Satan is on the cusp of giving them and the rest of the world a different story. He'll give them something to chew on; some answers and a good reason to hate Jehovah GOD and the Bible's version of Jesus Christ. He'll happily give the world a more suitable version of the Nazarene—the prophet. His five powerful and gifted demon-archangels are seeing to it; diligently and joyfully as they speak.

Ephesians 6:11-12 *For we do not wrestle against flesh and blood, but against principalities, against powers, against the rulers of the darkness of this world, against spiritual hosts of wickedness in the heavenly places.*

-Chapter Eleven-
SATAN'S GENERALS

In the tongue of Angels and Demons:
"Let them panic. Let them scream and squirm; these little cockroaches, dogs, and bitches of Jehovah." Vy-Apheélion voiced with elation and pleasure.

In the heart of Los Angeles, the powerful high-ranking demon and his underling in flight over the massive city, hovering here and there, bouncing from rooftop to rooftop watched the slurry of horrors beneath them with glee. It was sheer terror for the people, but for the demons; it was pure entertainment.

At the moment; atop the Hollywood Memorial Hospital, peering over the edges looking down on the mayhem and a world gone mad, Vy-Apheélion, in his hubris continued to comment.

"I never dreamed the Nazarene's Harvest would be so delightful and fun. It is good. It is very good — is

IT WAS A FREEWILL RAPTURE

it not Jur-Phalli?" he cheered with a menacing snicker.

"Delightful." Phalli said as the two of them savored the sight.

Without taking his eyes off what he was finding to be so amusing and agreeable, Vy-Apheélion continued to gloat and revel at the sight below. "Look at them." He spoke. "Look at them cringe. Look at them run — they're so pathetic. They don't even know what they're running from. Ahh yes, to watch them suffer. I never tire."

"How long, Master? How long are we to let them run in this season of torment?" Phalli asked out of curiosity.

"We are to let them quiver, let them cry, and curse a little longer, Jur-Phalli. Yes..., I'm told a little longer — orders from Lord-Lucifer. They need to suffer longer. The more they agonize, the more they are tormented and tortured the better. It will work to our advantage. Timing is everything." Apheélion stressed and repeated. "Timing is everything!"

Jur-Phalli, in good standing with his superior, listened with great interest. He was absorbed and extremely attracted to Vy-Apheélion's rank and wisdom; wisdom handed down from the top. He was learning. He was climbing the ranks himself.

In light of the latest developments, he was getting familiar with Lucifer's masterful tactics, his latest arrangements, plans and schemes so as to flaunt his authority, reclaim his dominion, and ultimately prove Jehovah God wrong. Vy-Apheélion, without reservation, (Vy-, a surname of the highest command; a General /Jur- a surname of a lower rank) continued to brief his loyal and inquisitive underling. He'd let Jur-Phalli in on what Satan told him directly.

"Like us, my good servant…, we need to let the other *principalities* of the highest order persist, to each their own dominion." Apheélion said. "We're to keep firewire on the blink; and the portals, signals and frequencies shut down; all except image capturing apparatus. Those…, as you know, we're not to touch and dare not disrupt.

"Why…, my Lord? Surveillance cameras and the tele-portals capturing our activity? Why do we keep the firewire alive in such matters? Phalli respectfully quizzed.

"Lord Lucifer has plans. He will use the footage to his gain in due time, shortly I might add. But now, we follow orders. We persist…! All of us…! Vy-Pécula, Vy-Fonteé, Vy-Gréthos, and Vy-Deélia…, they too are to keep the fire burning. And we don't stop until Lord Lucifer says enough!"

They did indeed persist; all five of Satan's highest, most powerful of principalities — the Generals. Vy-Pécula, lord of the elements; stirring the tempests, the

IT WAS A FREEWILL RAPTURE

winds, and earthquakes is to be unrelenting, as is Vy-Fonteé, lord of the Influencers; the dark messengers, like Dmitri. They haven't wasted a second worming their way into the minds of anyone having even the slightest chance of getting to know Jehovah God, Jesus Christ, or even the Bible itself. The minds they're sabotaging, the hearts they're poisoning with their special ability to whisper thoughts is vast and uncountable.

Vy-Apheélion, as he explained to his subordinate, is to continue tormenting the humankind with an erratic power grid. He's to keep on teasing them with power shortages, distorted frequencies and faulty satellite signals. Called Gremlins in fairytales; Apheélion's demons are cluttering the airwaves and taunting the people with little spurts of electricity here or a little spurt there, with flickering and dimming lights. They're playing with medical and security equipment, street lights, cell phones, computers; anything to make the sons and daughters of flesh and blood go crazy as they plummet into despair.

Vy-Gréthos, he who lords over the 'crossover demons', those who have the power to transcend and manifest in the third-dimension; he's been commanded to ramp up the UFO sightings. Lucifer needs him to make the sightings more plentiful and alluring to feed imaginations. The hour to unleash his army of 'crossovers demons' to their full capacity however is

DAVID ALAN SMITH

on hold for the time being. Soon, he'll get the green light to disperse his 'crossovers' into the world so as to interact with the masses on a more up-close and personal basis.

Vy-Gréthos has managed to do it over the centuries; get his crossover demons to interact with the humankind, but it was so limited—like a slow drip of a leaky faucet. But now, with the hand of the Holy Spirit that restrained him removed, Satan will have him pour his crossovers into the world like irrigating a field. It'll go far beyond an open faucet. It'll be closer to gushing wells and pouring rain.

The crossover demons interacting with humans will be plentiful. It'll be however strategic and masterfully regulated. There's a methodical and sinister agenda to maintain and like the other Generals of darkness, Vy-Gréthos knows he'd do well to stay on course. And that he'll do; even now—the surge and splendor of the UFO sightings peppering the skies has been enhanced as well as doubled.

As for Vy-Deélia...? He who lords over *'legion'*, the expendable ones; he's received new orders from Lucifer as well, to which Apheélion was excited to share with Jur Phalli. Vy-Apheélion knows via celestial telepathy, a gift to which only the higher demon-angels in rank and power possess. It's why the *powers of darkness* are so organized and able to intervene on

∽ 146 ∽

IT WAS A FREEWILL RAPTURE

matters in a moment's notice.

Updating Jur-Phalli, "Lucifer says our damage this day needs to be thorough, long lasting, and scarring." Apheélion explained. "And Vy- Deélia has been ordered to take the horrors to new heights."

Seeing the countenance on his master' face, Phalli smiled with anticipation. He knew Apheélion was thrilled. The blueish glow slightly generating on the tips of Apheélion majestic appendages; mainly on his fingers and wings was more than enough to verify his commander's delight. It was also enough to stir his curiosity.

"What, my lord? What is Vy-Deélia called to do that makes you grimace so…, and emit such joy?" Jur-Phalli egged.

With a wicked smile, "Vy-Deélia…, yes…, yes! He's not only commanded to persist, but he, my good servant, is to ratchet his dominion up another notch. He's been ordered to disperse the second round of 'legion' — to ramp up the possessions; more animal attacks and…, even more delightful, the flesh turning on their own will commence."

Pondering the update, Jur-Phalli offered his thoughts. "Is this perhaps what they've come to love and adore, Master? Have they not gazed at their portals and fixated on such horrors? Apocalyptic flesh-eating beasts and the walking dead? It'll serve these dogs well, will it not, my Lord—giving them a taste of their own entertainment?" Phalli asserted to please his superior.

Apheélion chuckled. "Yes…, a taste of their own; just a bit mind you—just a little taste. After that, my good servant, when Vy-Deélia's *'legion'* and the other dominions have run their course, then we'll be summoned to unblock the humans' measly little morsels of what they seem to think is…their…great power."

Jur Phalli knew exactly what Apheélion meant. 'The human's measly little morsels of what they seem to think is their 'great power' is none other than electricity and technology. The demons refer to it as 'firewire'.

Stupid ones…!" Apheélion jeered and laughed. "For these fools to think they have the means and ability to fix and restore the power grid is laughable. Yet…, we'll lead them to believe what they love to believe, Jur-Phalli. And yes…, my good servant…, they do indeed believe they have such power."

"Like the climate…?" Phalli said astutely.

"Ahh…, nicely put, Jur-Phalli…, yes—just like the Climate." Apheélion praised. "Well said. The arrogance Lucifer has sewn into their souls—is it not superb? These little know-nothing vermin who teach their young that they alone have the power to control the climate—as if they're the Most-High God

IT WAS A FREEWILL RAPTURE

themselves—what fools!" He raved.

"Even now...," Jur-Phalli added, "as Vy-Pécula persists, they believe the tempests and earthquakes ravaging them is their doing—'the fallout from them damaging the climate' they cry..., over and over."

Smirking, "Yes..., exactly how Lucifer planned it. It too will play into our hands." Apheélion assured and laughed with glee, finding it wickedly humorous.

Phalli obviously found it to be a laughable matter because he had to laugh at the thought, as did Apheélion, who went on to say, "Ahh..., the things we've gotten these arrogant idiots to believe—and so easily."

"Only to do it again, Master—make them think and believe it is they themselves who fix and restore the firewire?" Phalli asserted.

"Yes..., yes indeed. They'll pat themselves on the back, believing they, in all their genius, stabilized the power grid. Is it not infuriating that we're called to make them believe such nonsense?" Apheélion scowled and continued to rave.

"Do they not know it is now...I...and my dominion that opens the faucet and closes the faucet—to give them the firewire or deprive them of it? Do they not know that it is now...I...who controls the airwaves and energy—who gives life to their portals; the idol to which I've given them to worship?" He clamored,

∽ 149 ∽

almost angry that the people know nothing of the kind.

The blueish glow of delight instantly morphed into a softer red; hinting anger on the rise. The thought of him having to keep his power under wraps irked him so. Jur-Phalli has witnessed his disgust many, many times.

"Keeping these pathetic creatures in the dark and clueless as to who we are and the power we possess is grating, Jur-Phalli. I hate it…!"

"Yet…, we know why—do we not?" Phalli reminded.

"Yes…, yes we do—Hail Lucifer." Apheélion acknowledged, knowing quite well why they remain in the shadows of darkness.

"In due time though," he added as he calmed down. "They'll find out soon enough that it is we who own everything they hold dear. For now, although sickening—we'll patronize them as Lord Lucifer commands."

Continuing, "We'll flick on their portals, restore their firewire to its full capacity, open their channels of communication, and replenish the air waves. We shall give these feeble 'children of flesh' the impression they've restored all energy, and they'll feverishly watch the very things we've given them to enslave them.

IT WAS A FREEWILL RAPTURE

Thus, all these worthless, mangy dogs and bitches will get what they want—some answers. Yet, they'll know not, the answers they get will be as it's always been..., what is *'falsely called knowledge'*."

"How long..., Master?" Phalli asked, "How long before we open their lines of communication and disperse the information; give them visuals on their portals?"

"Soon..., soon enough! For now, though, let us first enjoy the other *principalities* taunt and tease the prey. Vy-Deélia's *'legion'* is most amusing. Henceforth, communication will begin on a moment's notice upon Lucifer's command. Then we shall feed them. We feed them what we want them to know. But now..., for the time being Phalli, my good servant—we wait. Yes..., we wait indeed." Vy-Apheélion pressed.

Everything went as planned. Capitalizing on the Nazarene's Harvest, Satan in all of his otherworldly genius was as much methodical as he was prompt. He not only knew exactly when, but exactly how much and where to unleash the immense power under his command.

Brilliance on display; Vy-Deélia's second round of *Legion* was deployed. The demon possessions increased. In turn, not only did the animal attacks

DAVID ALAN SMITH

double, but people were now being possessed — taking the living nightmare from bad to worse.

The 'expendable ones', the demons of *'legion'* already swarming the face of the planet like locusts didn't hesitate to move in and possess all those already susceptible to them; those of whom the demons refer to as the 'opened vessels.' It took nothing at all to enter them, and of course control them. From that point, it wasn't only animals people needed to beware and fear; it was now other people.

Compelled by the powers of darkness, led by… *spiritual hosts of wickedness in the Heavenly places…*, 'unclean spirits' as the Bible puts it, the demon possessed people would align with the crazed blood-thirsty possessed animals and boost the number of fatalities across the globe. Unusually enlarged pupils, and protruding; making their eye's look like black buttons on top of pools of broken blood vessels, frothing at the mouth, adrenaline peaked — the souls controlled by *'legion'* fearlessly attacked onlookers like crazed zombies.

It was right out of the movies, only it wasn't a movie this time. It was real; as it was in the Gospels. It was the same *'unclean spirits'*…, the same demonic possession of people and animals; just a different time.

In a matter of hours, the possessed were already being killed by the thousands as they themselves

IT WAS A FREEWILL RAPTURE

killed thousands more with their brutal attacks. In the streets, in the gatherings and shelters, in churches, even in the households and homes, within families; for all those having to contend with the possessed monsters ravaging civilization, it was kill-or-be-killed.

Killing them was seemingly the only thing to do, even the right thing to do. People really didn't have much of a choice. Any attempt to subdue those possessed with the *unclean spirits* or overpower them; to pin them down, tie them up, lock them up, to restrain them so as to take them alive was near impossible. Being the police in every corner of the world already depleted and Martial Law not yet fully implemented, it was mostly citizens and family members taking down the vicious and brutal zombie-like savages.

Emboldened with uninhibited rage, empowered with superhuman strength, extremely fast, sadistic and violent, they'd attack anyone and everyone on sight. Using anything they could get their hands on, they'd butcher, bludgeon, and kill anybody they'd see; even their own family. If no weapon was readily available, they'd go to wildly biting, scratching and clawing, and gouging and punching until the killing was complete. The only thing that separated them from the movies is they didn't stop to eat their kill. They speedily rushed to kill another and another.

The multitudes already in shock by the Rapture;

the terrifying moments of being held in place, the vanishings, more especially the children, and pregnancies coming to nothing—now they were finding themselves having to fight for their lives on top of it all.

As Apheélion knew it would be, it was a sight to see. The *powers of darkness* of all classes and ranks were enjoying every second of it. To each their own.

As for Satan..., he too would relish the peaking hours. He would so love to take the horrors he's relentlessly inflicting on humanity over the passing hours further, but it would go against his better judgment. It would topple his bigger motive; hinder is newborn agenda.

For now, like his generals, he'll just savor the moment until it's time to go into phase-two of his grand scheme.

Mark 5:1-13 *'And when Jesus stepped out of the boat, immediately there met Him out of the tombs a man with an evil spirit, who had his dwelling among the tombs; and no one could bind him, not even with chains, because he had often been bound with shackles and chains. And the chains had been pulled apart by him, and the shackles broken in pieces; neither could anyone tame him. And always, night and day, he was in the mountains and in the tombs, crying out and cutting himself with stones.*

When he saw Jesus from afar, he ran and fell down before Him. And he cried out with a loud voice and said, "What have I to do with You, Jesus, Son of the Most-High God? I beg You, do not torment me!" For Jesus had said to him, "Come out of this man, you evil spirit!" Then Jesus asked him, "What is your name?"

And he answered, saying, "My name is Legion; for we are many." And he begged Jesus again and again not to send them out of the realm.

Now a large herd of pigs was feeding there near the mountains. So, all the demons begged Jesus, "Send us to the pigs, that we may enter them." And at once Jesus gave them permission. Then the evil spirits went out and entered the pigs (there were about two thousand); and the herd ran violently down the steep hillside into the sea, and drowned.'

-Chapter Twelve-
THE WALKING DEAD

The 'open vessels'...; after Vy-Deélia's *'legion'* effortlessly entered and possessed them, they may as well be dead. Their fate was already sealed by their own hand. It would be all those who had already plunged into the deeper and darker pools of the Occult and Witchcraft; who had willfully given their souls over to Satan and other demons summoned by name.

It was only the open vessels that *'legion'* and the *'evil and unclean spirits'* were able to possess, besides the animals. In the grand scheme of things, there was only a small swath of the sons and daughters of the humankind deliberately worshipping the devil in the world, but plenty enough to forge a small army strewn about the globe.

Up to now, Satan's earthly followers assumed it well to do his bidding over the years. From the most famous of rock and hip-hop artists, pop idols, and movie stars to the least of covens and loyal loners; Satan found their devotion and service to be quite useful and amusing. The wealthiest of moguls and royalty who sold their souls to Satan were most beneficial. Their money, power, and influence to advance the

IT WAS A FREEWILL RAPTURE

powers of darkness were invaluable to he who owned them.

Serving him was no small matter. Hate God..., hate Jesus...; spurn the Christians and Zionists, lambast the Bible and the Gospel, only to bow down and worship him—give their lives over to him—what more could Satan want of them? His loyal servants however had no idea their Lord of Darkness had one more thing for them to do.

The Nazarene's Harvest ushered in a new era for the devil; a different kind of war. It spawned a new agenda. As odd as it sounds, the new war on all things that are God and Jesus would have no place for the Satan Worshippers of old. They would be conflicting and troublesome; more of a hindrance than a service in the devil's newest campaign.

It's time for a new breed of worshippers. He doesn't want—nor has he ever wanted a near insignificant little sect of people to worship him as the devil—a mere angel. This is insulting. What he wants is a world to worship him as 'God'. This is the desire, and this is his chance. Thus, certain things need to be done.

Long planned, getting rid of the devout Satanists was clearly Satan's best option. Devil Worshippers, along with their pentagrams, sacrificial ceremonies, and shrines of Alester Crowley espousing "Do What Thy Wilt" dogma; they just wouldn't fit in the new kingdom Satan has in mind. Those bound to worshipping the universal personification of what is pure evil and darkness cannot mix with those who'll believe they're worshipping the light that has come to save them.

Satan knows if he's to be like the Most-High God, his new breed of worshippers and god-seekers would find it repulsive to know they were somehow connected to the devil worshippers of old. It would be a blot on his new kingdom. They'll only poison the well; a well that is prepped and ready to quench the people's thirst with a new kind of darkness.

With that, it was time to remove the traditional devil worshippers. It was time to rid them like infected rats, but not without first being of service. Seeing they were at the end of their reign and expendable, Satan would use his subservient pawns one last time to accelerate his quest to be the world's new God. Possessing them, so as to turn them into crazed, bloodthirsty fiends and monsters ravaging the world like a plague; it'll be just one more thing people will count as a blessing from God when the carnage comes to a halt; of which he cleverly intends to do.

For now, though, to see his little army of foolish, but loyal followers of old on the warpath and getting wiped out at the same time was most delightful. There was no love lost; not a single iota as far as Satan was

IT WAS A FREEWILL RAPTURE

concerned. How could there be when there was no love for them in the first place?

When it came to the fallen angel and his sentiments toward the sons and daughters of God's Creation; it was the purest of pure hatred for them, all of them, even those who thought it well to worship him. It could be said, he loved their devout adoration, but he didn't love them—at all.

It's the worship that he'd get from them that he craved. It's what he feeds on; gets high on. Having been so madly in love with the reverence and glory he'd get from the tiny little sect of devil worshippers, how much more will he love the entire world worshipping him at his feet? It is the day he's dreamed of. He got close in the days of Noah, but it was snuffed out—actually flooded out.

At this point, it was only the beginning of his dastardly mission; a most methodical one at that. Henceforth, the horror continued for hours on in. Vy-Deélia's power and control over *'legion'* was strong and impressive. The demonic possession over the animals and Satan's worshippers of old were clearly taking the international madness to new heights.

The earthquakes and tremors worldwide, although mild, were most intimidating. They were nonstop; Vy-Pécula and his demons over the elements were seeing to that. Adding the raging winds and the stormy conditions only embellished the tremors. It was ominous and led many to believe it was surely the end of the world.

Vy-Gréthos 'crossover demons' sporadically manifesting as UFO's swarming around like phantoms and wasps; that and Vy-Fonteé's Influencers toying with uncountable minds stirred imaginations to no end. They planted doubts, anger, and hate in the hearts of millions already poisoned with fear and agony. They drove many to suicide and many more insane.

All that on top of the children disappearing, and all pregnancies ceasing to exist. The mentally blameless and selective Christians vanishing as well only made things even more confusing and chaotic. Words couldn't describe the madness; it was beyond words. Had the people not been watching it all happen right before their eyes and experiencing it firsthand it'd be beyond belief. Even then, even being in the thick of it was impossible to fathom, let alone comprehend.

Vy-Apheélion keeping the firewire at bay was a brilliant touch, but more so very important. Satan knows its power over the people; their addiction to it. He should. Like a shrewd, conniving drug dealer, he's the one who methodically got them addicted to it and their portals; almost to the point of worshipping them.

A world in crisis without the convenience and abundance of electricity, phones, televisions, and

IT WAS A FREEWILL RAPTURE

mass communications at their fingertips was proving to be extremely advantageous when it came to driving people over the edge. As is with any drug dealer, the people's dependency on firewire and portals is a wonderful thing to he who has the power to control its distribution and flow.

They need the drugs, and Satan knows their need goes on to say they need the drug dealer; of whom they'll eventually put on a pedestal to worship. Soon..., he figures—very soon. But, not yet.

Still, even without the people worshipping him as of yet, he was feeling more and more like the Most-High God with each passing minute. With himself on the throne and his Generals mimicking the power of God at his command; he was quickly getting used to it. Even though the people weren't yet worshipping him as God, in his own twisted way, they were crying out to him, begging him to stop all the post-Rapture horrors he's inflicting on them. And that, he'll do; and in turn give them something, or someone to worship and praise.

Hence, in a short while, Satan will give the anguished world a new and different path to salvation. He's already briefed his Vy Commanders that the hour to proceed is nearing. Until then, they need only to savor the moment; enjoy themselves watching the loathsome humankind suffer and lose their minds.

DAVID ALAN SMITH

Some fought for their lives; others ran for their lives. They frantically searched for their missing children and loved ones. People trembled and cowered, recoiled, and hid. There were those who gave into exhaustion; they buckled and fell. Many just grew numb and shut down, while others raced to suicide. But the demons...; those who never tire or sleep..., they rejoiced.

Rejoicing indeed. Now perched in the lower tiers of the Eiffel Tower; still being entertained at the havoc in the streets below, Vy-Apheélion abruptly jumped to attention.

"It's time...!" he vigorously said to Phalli at his side.

Out of the blue, in an instant, Apheélion took in a command directly from Lucifer via their celestial telepathy. With undivided attention, carefully listening to everything he was to promptly do; Apheélion would waste no time to carry out his orders.

"It's time. It's time to crack open the grid." He announced. "Time to feed the dogs, Jur-Phalli. The hour has come to give these creatures a feast. Go...!" Apheélion ordered. "Gather your regiments, scour the realm and align the command. Remove the barriers and blockage. The firewire will flow. Get as many portals opened up as fast as you can, but listen..., listen carefully! Keep their telecommunications at bay. We're not ready for vast interaction amongst the flesh at this

IT WAS A FREEWILL RAPTURE

point; not yet — not at this time." He firmly asserted.

Phalli respectfully looked puzzled, yet anxious to carry out his superiors' command. Seeing his servant's silent inquiry, Apheélion quickly enlightened him.

"We need a season of their undivided attention, Phalli." He explained. "We need these fools to sit there and gawk at their portals, to be still and fixate on the magnitude of our power before they start flapping their tongues — of things they know nothing about."

Continuing, "Exchanging thoughts beyond earshot is prohibited until they fully understand the carnage happening outside their doors is happening on the other side of the world. It is time for them to eat the feast we give them on their portals; time for them to eat, Phalli — not speak! This…, my good servant, is why we've been ordered to open the portals only and keep mass communication at a standstill. Do you understand?' He sternly asked, bordering on intimidation.

Phalli would get it. He would not only get it, he liked it. Now on the same page and eager to do his part, "The portals, Master…., the entire sphere…?" Phalli asked.

"Yes…, open it up…, all of it…, even their hand-portals! Unleash their mind-controlling boxes. Unclog and revamp their firewires and airwaves. We need to show them how much they need a Savior…; a God to tickle their desires and quench their thirst for answers."

∽ 163 ∽

DAVID ALAN SMITH

Aroused and impressed with Lucifer's masterful tactics; Jur-Phalli immediately moved to carry out the command. Finally, after a day and a half; thirty-three some odd hours or so after the Rapture, everything that had to do with Vy-Apheélion's dominion over electricity, airwaves and signals were loosened.

Considering the world's addiction to firewire and their portals; Satan allowing Vy-Apheélion to open it up, even just a part of it, was like a fix, or perhaps a stiff drink in the trembling hands of a severe alcoholic. An addiction or not, the information highway was finally opened up so as to feed the masses their feast of happenings across the globe.

With the portals unlocked, from smartphones to televisions, and everything in between; the multitudes wallowing in fear were sure to get a better idea of just how devastating and terrifying the crisis is, as well as how thorough and far-reaching it is.

It wouldn't be answers, at least not the kind people were praying for. Not yet—Satan made that very clear. The answers given this hour are more about the extent of what's happening, as opposed to why it was happening…, or who's behind it. He'll be handing out those answers soon enough. He'll give them all the answers they want, so as to give them plenty of good reasons to want him.

They will be his people, and he will be their God;

IT WAS A FREEWILL RAPTURE

as the Bible puts it. Only it's Jehovah God the scriptures are speaking of, but who's to say? Certainly not those unfamiliar with the Bible. At this point, as frail and vulnerable as the people are...; Satan stepping into an imitation of God's shoes is already proving to be a cinch. And he's only beginning.

And so it went. Vy-Apheélion's limitless army of demonic gremlins; they'd stand down and allow the firewire to flow and the airwaves and satellite signals through. The connections were made, thus in turn; the media was up and running. News commentators, reporters and endless video footage from the surveillance cameras and phones came pouring out of the portals for all to see.

And yet, mass telecommunication was stifled; regulated to a bare minimum. Even so, likened to Randy being overjoyed to finally hear his radio kick on during his trip from hell, the world too was overjoyed to finally see their phones and TV's coming back to life after being dead for so long. It was a one-way street; receiving information with zero interaction, but it was still a relief; more of a blessing really.

How kind and generous of the devil to give them such a wonderful treat? There were plenty who were quick to say 'Thank, God'. The question is...; which God do they thank?

1 Thessalonians 4:16-18 *For the Lord Himself will come down from heaven, and with a loud command, with the voice of the archangel and with the trumpet call of God, and the dead in Christ will rise first. After that, we who are still alive and are left will be caught up together with them in the clouds to meet the Lord in the air. And so, we will be with the Lord forever. Therefore, encourage each other with these words.*

⚘

-*Chapter Thirteen*-

HERE'S THE NEWS

"We do not know…, nor have we confirmed anyone who does know what is behind the catastrophic events," would stream out of a barely known anchorman brandishing a thick British accent. "What we do know is the bizarre attacks; the vanishings, sightings, earthquakes and unusual weather patterns are global in nature—as is the technical difficulties."

Barry Bona; direct, clear and proper would speak with great concern, but overly robust, he was not. It isn't to say he was dry and robotic; like the emotionless loop on Randy's radio, it's just his countenance seemed somewhat detached. Clearly, he wasn't one

IT WAS A FREEWILL RAPTURE

who had lost a child or dealing with the death of someone close or even attacked by some crazed animal or a possessed knife-wielding maniac. It was just the impression Randy would get as he, Becky and Jake watched attentively.

Everybody would be watching someone somewhere sharing the details and grateful for it. It was because they were starving for info; as Satan intended them to be. The only thing that's even come remotely close to all eye's glued to their TV's and phones was watching the first men and women astronauts landing on Mars. As big as the historical event was, it was dwarfed by the number of people watching the media at this hour.

Clearly, the stream of broadcasts went a lot further than just another day of the anchors reciting 'Here's the news'. To think it a new day fashioning the latest news wasn't even on the radar. Today's broadcast was, in a sense, like a new birth.

For the very first time, the media would begin to address a world without the Holy Spirit of God and void of the Born-Again Christians. It would begin to address a world without the innocence of younger children, toddlers, babies, and mentally blameless souls. Lastly, it would address a world left without a single woman pregnant.

Being the skies were peppered with intermittent

∽ 167 ∽

DAVID ALAN SMITH

UFO sightings and the entire world suddenly plagued with crazed people inexplicably attacking and butchering anyone they set their eyes on, even their own family; they too were a first for the media. The only experience they had is what they learned from the movies; of which paled to what they're experiencing at the moment.

Regardless, Barry Bona continued uninterrupted. He was by far the most watched of all the commentators; mostly because the network he was on is so far-reaching and popular. The IBN; the International Broadcasting Network is just that..., an international broadcast; easily and readily available on every format; smartphones, TV's, computers, live-stream, etc., etc. But, Mr Bona, himself needed to take a little credit for being the most watched.

Even though he's always been nothing more than a fill-in anchorman, like a substitute teacher, hardly known, he was apparently hand-picked to take on the role of being the world's anchorman; at least for the time being. All the other more famous anchors on the network were too discombobulated and frantic to address an already frightened and panic-stricken world. Their professionalism failed to live up to the crisis at hand. But, Bona—he was for the most part very measured; balanced, you might say..., calm, but aggressive. It helped the grieving viewers tremendously to

IT WAS A FREEWILL RAPTURE

see a little composure in the midst of all the chaos.

No matter who'd be reporting; in one form or another from one source or another, details came pouring out of every available portal. All peoples were getting more familiar with the impact the Rapture had on the world. Slowly but surely, a picture would be painted for all to see. For the history books, the facts would finally emerge.

Late winter..., 2043; it was Tuesday morning, February 29th, 6:26 a.m. Pacific Standard Time that the world plunged headfirst into its nightmare. No choice in the matter, by force; all life was thrust into a different kind of world — one that could only have been imagined.

The Rapture, now coined the Mass Vanishing by secular standards happened simultaneously. Spanning across the globe; the event was synchronized to the very second. What happened at 6:26 AM in California happened at 3:26 PM in London and 11:26 PM on the coast of Japan.

An unprecedented amount of surveillance and video footage abroad spoke volumes. It showed everything; that is to say everything outside of what's being called the "lost 2 ½ minutes". None of the Rapture was caught on tape. Footage showing all things held in place was not recorded. In essence, for whatever reasons, the Rapture itself was limited to eyewitness

DAVID ALAN SMITH

accounts and eyewitness accounts only.

All video footage showed the 'east to west' strike of lightening and, as if edited, the next available frame would be the 'instant release'. The very moment the cameras clicked back on was the moment all things mysteriously held in place by unseen forces broke free. It was as if the whole world was put on pause, yet it wasn't; things happened.

The billions of video recording sources, equipment and cameras across the world weren't scrambled for 2 ½ minutes, they just stopped recording. Like the people, along with all facets of transportation from planes, helicopters, jets and drones to bicycles, escalators, and cars, on down to bullets, flyballs at baseball games and mosquitos; all video recording too was paused until the prophetic Rapture fulfilled its calling. It was 2 minutes 33 seconds to be exact.

Immediately after the lost 2 ½ minutes, from that point on; everything would be documented and confirmed. The surveillance and video footage would cover the aftermath in great detail. It gave the media, the reporters, and anchors an endless list of things to report on. Its haunting footage showed everything.

"It cannot…, it just cannot be denied!" Bona emphasized with great intensity. "People and children have simply vanished; leaving nothing but a pile of whatever attire they had on at the time of their

IT WAS A FREEWILL RAPTURE

abduction. Where they've gone and who or what has taken them is not yet known, but we see the footage, they're gone." He drilled.

Clothes, jewelry, wigs and hairpieces, fake fingernails, everything; even down to the unseen remnants of ink from tattoos all lay as they would be dropped to the ground where they departed. Anything that wasn't of their natural body lay discarded. There were reports of prosthetics, hearing aids, identification microchips, braces, fillings, stitches, contact lens, bandages and medical appendages from metal plates to pacemakers and pliable tubing, even organ transplants as well as undigested food all lay where they may, lifeless and valueless to all those who were gloriously taken in the Rapture.

For some, however, the belongings may have laid dormant and lifeless, but definitely not valueless. For it didn't take long for a certain mentality to take advantage of the alluring and vulnerable treasures left at their fingertips. Randy saw it first hand when the kid didn't hesitate to pick up the diamond ring and necklace and put it in his pocket. But, the video footage and reporting on it painted a far better picture of it than Randy's testimony could have ever done.

Sadly, within minutes it seemed, as frightening and peculiar as it was, amidst all the screams and cries and the pandemonium that had instantly seized control of

DAVID ALAN SMITH

the air, there were those who just couldn't resist the temptation. Though a little hesitant and awkward at first, but not restrained, those who had lost nothing and had nothing to lose did not waste any time to rummage through the defenseless belongings full of riches laying at their disposal in the public streets and facilities.

Having only to keep a watchful eye out for the crazed animals and possessed people, the opportunists had a field day. Taking anything and everything of value served their unsavory conscience well. Crazed themselves, unconcerned and totally aloof to the higher meaning and impact behind the miraculous disappearance of so many people...; pillaging lifeless piles of clothes for treasure seemed to be more important.

As long as the lifeless piles laid unattended and publicly visible, and the longer they would lie, the more they would be ransacked. It didn't take long before all of the inert piles of what had once been someone's personal belongings were plundered, scattered and discarded all over the place.

Ransacking piles of lifeless clothes wasn't the only thing that was taking the world by storm. Like a raging fire, the looting soon turned the corner and started to fan into higher end stores and malls; even homes. Setting their sights on costly merchandise, the people simply started to rush into the stores and

IT WAS A FREEWILL RAPTURE

break storefront windows to get their hands on the valuables. TV's, smartphones, laptops, jewelry, video game consoles, clothing, appliances; even cars, motorcycles, trucks, and motor homes—anything that had a lucrative price tag flaunting dollars and cents was up for grabs. And in the eyes of the hunters, the higher the tag—the better.

Self-indulgence however was only part of the tornado of people sweeping the streets on a crazed and wide-eyed scavenger hunt. Unlike the looters compelled by the spirit of greed, the spirit of survival was even stronger. It was "end of the world" lunacy.

Thousands upon thousands of people spontaneously clicked into survival mode and in droves, they raced and forced their way into grocery stores, and convenient stores, and department stores, and drug stores; any store or facility that carried food and water so as to round up as much and as many provisions as they possibly could and as fast as they could. Within a matter of hours, if not minutes, the countless shelves across the world that had neatly assembled goods for sale were picked clean and torn apart.

The frenzied harvest for merchandise, food, water and other survival provisions didn't go without its share of violence and casualties. People just went nuts. The fighting and scrapping, often to the point of brutality and even death was endless. Fueled by selfish

∞ 173 ∞

ambition, almost trance-like, likened to the demon-possessed, the people hungrily snatched and grabbed anything and everything they could possibly carry, either off the shelves or from each other.

There were some noble and respectful enough to make concerted and half-hearted efforts to discipline or discourage the crazed robbers, but it was to no avail. It had in fact become dangerous; and then stupid and foolish to even try. It wasn't long before the curtains of apathy closed on their concern, even for the local authorities and law enforcement. There was just too much going on; too much going too fast.

The noise was intense. Immediately after the Rapture; alarms, sirens, horns and screams pierced the air and instantly conquered every single domain harboring serenity and silence. Everywhere, people were panic-stricken and recklessly running around yelling and wailing at the top of their lungs. Even on the most remote of islands and desolate of habitats, the screams alone of people dealing with missing children, lost loved ones and animal attacks were deafening. In the more congested areas, sporadic explosions and municipal utility and power grid failures were unrelenting.

Fires had broken out all over the place. Emergency units were depleted, hospitals and clinics were overrun, and law enforcement was flat out overwhelmed.

IT WAS A FREEWILL RAPTURE

There were casualties and fatalities on every corner. Dead bodies from all the accidents, demonic attacks and fighting were uncountable. As for the difference between the dead bodies that lay strewn about and the bodies that disappeared, it left everyone to wonder.

Traffic in metropolitan areas was piled up beyond measure. A good part of the people who found themselves hopelessly frozen and wedged in the traffic had set their sights on getting out of Dodge, if you will. For them, it was proving to be a miserable mistake. The streets and highways came to dead halts. They were stuck, and to abandon their vehicles was to abandon their valuables, rations and supplies.

There were others caught in the stagnant mess who were fixated on something far more important than just getting out of Dodge though. So much so that they didn't think twice about abandoning their vehicles right where they stood in traffic. Leaving them to the fate of thievery, vandals and impounds, these particular people weren't just hurried; they were desperate.

On foot, feverishly racing, meandering and pounding their way through the onslaught of bumper-to-bumper traffic, they were determined; and for good reason. It had nothing to do with running away from the rampant bedlam; they had their sights set on something else. It was their homes, their families and loved ones that they were nervously trying to get to.

DAVID ALAN SMITH

It was all that mattered and all they cared about. Who could blame them?

The news got out quick about the missing children; even with the firewire, telecommunications, and signals shut down. Word of mouth swept the streets like a range fire. The missing adults were one thing, but the children…? When it got out that the children were targeted, that was it. Hysteria jumped a thousand-fold.

Everyone watching and absorbing all the terrifying footage and reports were sickened. Those grieving, like Becky and Jake would only grieve more. Those frightened, like Nicki Dawn, Chad and their friends only became more fearful. Sadly…, there were also those who just couldn't handle it. As the hours passed, suicides surged.

Uncertainty would only deepen in the minds of those like Randy and Leah watching one report after another. Even Leah, who knew it was the Rapture, was having a difficult time wrapping her arms around all the atrocities and peculiarities ravaging the earth in its aftermath. She didn't know what to think.

There were others though who weren't at all confused or mystified. Attentively observing the rise in anxiety and desperation go through the roof, Jur-Phalli could only reflect and smile on what Vy-Apheélion told him.

'We need a season of their undivided attention. We

IT WAS A FREEWILL RAPTURE

need these fools to sit there and gawk at their portals, to be still and fixate on the magnitude of our power before they start flapping their tongues—of things they know nothing about. It is time for them to eat the feast we give them on their portals; time for them to eat—not speak.'

To see the methodical phase in his Lord Lucifers' plan perfectly executed was most impressive; and beautiful, Jur-Phalli thought. His master is nurturing them, is how he saw it. Like baby birds, feed them first and then set them free to fly. It was amazing, because the people were doing just that. Instead of jiggling up and down with open beaks though, it was their minds—and they were feverishly swallowing everything that came pouring out of their portals.

Oddly enough; and as Satan expected, the only comfort anyone had was knowing they weren't alone in all this madness. It seemed to help. To think the entire planet from continent to continent was consumed and cast into the same incomprehensible whirlwind of emotional trauma and world devastation forged a sense of unity and togetherness.

It's perfect, though. Unity and togetherness…? 'Imagine all the people, living life as one'…? Satan couldn't ask for a better scenario. Everybody on the same page is exactly what he will need if he's to succeed. For he knows he cannot tout the Holy Scripture;

DAVID ALAN SMITH

'*They will be my people..., and I will be their God.*', if unity and togetherness isn't burnt into the hearts of his subjects. That, he intends to do—and is in fact doing at this very moment as he feeds his 'baby birds' all the things they'll need to be of one mind, one heart, and of one spirit.

At this point, after a good five and half hours, Barry Bona and the rest of the anchors had pretty much given a watchful world a thorough report regarding the Mass Vanishing. There were a few surprises; some unexpected reports on some other matters.

Apparently, President Manning was hospitalized and reported to be in critical condition. Deedee..., the First Family's once friendly and playful sheepdog viciously attacked and mauled the President. The Secret Service was caught off-guard, they never saw it coming. Also, a worldwide ceasefire was thought to be in effect. Wars and global indifferences; both, small and great, isolated and abroad would for the most part come to a halt. It was part of the world's sense of being in this mess together; a time to unite—perfect.

Other than that, the only thing left for Barry Bona and the rest of the media was to continue running footage on top of footage of new video's streaming in. It was the same with social media. On and on it went; a continuous run of unedited and graphic videos showing everything from the bloodcurdling animal attacks

IT WAS A FREEWILL RAPTURE

and homicidal rampages by the demon-possessed, to countless footage capturing UFO sightings and the weird and ominous weather patterns.

"Yes…, it is as Vy-Apheélion said it would be." Jur-Phalli preached to his own regiment of subordinates accompanying him as they made the rounds. Snickering with a smirk of content, "Is it not just that — a feast? Soon, they'll be filled and the fatted calf will be ours to devour."

Had anyone known there was some truth in the 'Hansel and Gretel' fairytale, it might have had more of an impact. The sweet, little ol' wicked witch with ulterior motives; methodically fattening Hansel so as to eat him really wasn't that far off from Jur-Phalli's comment. The only difference is, Satan is not going to be tricked and pushed into the oven by a couple of clever children who's on to him; mainly because the world has no idea what they're dealing with.

As it has always been.

Isaiah 14-14 *How you are fallen from heaven, O Lucifer, son of the morning!*

How you are cut down to the ground, you who weakened the nations!

For you have said in your heart:

'I will ascend into heaven…, I will exalt my throne above the stars of God;

I will also sit on the mount of the congregation; On the farthest sides of the north;

I will ascend above the heights of the clouds,

I will be like the Most-High.'

-Chapter Fourteen-
THIS GOD, THAT GOD

"Mom…, what is all this?" Nicki demanded. Like everyone else, she was dumbfounded. "Is this God? Is God doing all this?"

As her and Leah nervously sat there on the couch watching the endless news footage, reports and testimonies revealing one horrific nightmare after another, what else is Nicki to think? What else is there for anyone to think? Everybody knew they were dealing with a higher power; one they've never seen outside

IT WAS A FREEWILL RAPTURE

of movies, and there was nothing pretty or nice about it—let alone entertaining.

Wrath..., judgment..., an invasion..., aliens..., cosmic justice..., punishment for environmental abuse, even the end of the world was on the tip of everybody's tongues. It was in everybody's minds. The 'End of Days' and apocalyptic scenarios were the only conclusions of which there'd be no escape.

Topping everything off, everybody was helpless; even the most powerful of militaries across the world. How could they take a stand or form a line of defense against something they couldn't see? It would be like fighting the air. In a sense, it was exactly that—fighting the air. There's credence to Satan being referred to as the *'prince of the air'* in the Bible.

Still, the people didn't know who or what they were dealing with, or fighting with, or to whom they were pleading for mercy. They didn't know where to turn, what to do, who to address or even how to address this higher power, this unseen force letting the world know just how puny and powerless they really are and have always been.

God...? Crying out to God was the rampant and natural response, but as always and typical of a world blessed with the freewill and power to either fabricate the truth or adhere to the truth—who is God?

Figments of imagination, wishful thinking, the

DAVID ALAN SMITH

karmic universe, an impersonal force, some sort of energy, gods of this and gods of that, home-made gods, female gods, customized gods, Brahman, Gaia, Allah, an advanced Celestial Civilization from another galaxy—calling out to God went right back into calling out to whatever was in the mind of the beholder.

Of course, Jehovah—the God that gave this world the Bible, the God of Abraham, Isaac and Jacob; this God would of course be in the mix of people crying out to God. But this God, the God of all Creation, the God of Adam and Eve and Noah's Ark, the God that parted the Red Sea, the God that ordained the Virgin Birth, the God that walked on water, raised the dead and washed the feet of men; this God had stepped aside.

The Resurrected Christ, the Sacrificial Lamb of God being God Himself, the God that promised a Second Coming, who foretold and fulfilled the prophecy of the Rapture, God the Father, God the Son and God the Holy Spirit, the...MOST HIGH...; this God, yes..., most definitely was in the mix of people crying out to God, but by how many and for how long was up to the test.

Leah would answer Nicki's frantic question. In a near trance, distant and staring at the television, at the moment gawking at a horrific slice of news footage of people being devoured by sharks after a couple whales

IT WAS A FREEWILL RAPTURE

pummeled and sank their small yacht, she slowly and somberly uttered, "No Nicki…, this isn't God. God is gone."

It was a depressing answer, almost hopeless sounding. Even though she was seemingly in a daze, Leah was quite aware. She was also frightened. She was frightened for Nicki…; for the whole world, for that matter.

How were they ever going to believe that God isn't behind all of these demonic attacks on humanity. Of course, it was only her faith and her trust in the Bible that moved her to suggest it wasn't God. She knew the scriptures, and there was one in particular that just wouldn't stop pricking her brain.

"God would send strong delusion, that they should believe the lie" was the scripture. And here it was, up front and center, she figured. The…*strong delusion…* was already playing on Nicki.

As for God sending it…, it wasn't so much about Him sending it as it was Him allowing it. God was surely, but indirectly, behind all this madness Leah thought. It was only because God…, as He promised…, said the day will come; a day to which He'd remove Himself, His Spirit and His Church—ushering in the last days. Nobody knew what that was going to look like; that is until now. The day has come and the gates of hell were now open—wide open.

∽ 183 ∽

With the thought bouncing around in Leah's mind, along with watching all the horrors going down, she quietly mumbled…, really just talking to herself. "The only thing God had to do was step aside."

"What…?" Nicki challenged. She didn't quite catch it, but really it was more about losing her patience.

With a weighty sigh and eyes still glazed, staring at the TV, "Ahh…, nothing—" Leah moaned somberly.

It just sort of hit her at that moment, she realized nothing's changed. Thinking about Nicki's question, wondering if God is behind all these atrocities, troubled her. It wasn't so much about the question, or Nicki's bewilderment, as it was realizing her precious daughter is still in great danger. Even though she's been told numerous times over, even by Joel on some occasions; Nicki still hasn't grasped the fact there are two higher powers in this world…, and only two…; GOD and the devil—of whom the Bible refers to as '*the god of this age*'.

"Lord…," Leah silently prayed. How's she ever going to break down the walls in Nicki's mind; rip the blinders from her eyes to actually see and truly know these two higher powers are the difference between Light and Darkness, Truth and Lies, Life and Death, Winners and Losers, Heaven and Hell, and Salvation and Damnation?

But then, she realized she needn't look any further

IT WAS A FREEWILL RAPTURE

than herself and ask—how did she come to understand this invisible war? She really didn't know the answer. It's a mysterious thing—to be *'born again'*.

What she did know; along with a loving God, a glorious Savior, and an all-encompassing Holy Spirit, there were plenty of prayers from many people that her eyes be opened. She could only resort to that; and she has and will continue to pray for Nicki. She'll continue to do everything she can to share the Word of God every chance she gets as well.

To see Nicki Dawn cross over the threshold that converts her from one who's merely informed about the invisible war into one who knows it to be true with every fiber of their being is a day she longs for. But that hour has not yet come. And to know it might not ever come is the kicker.

She knows the *'power of darkness'*; that it's strong as much as it is alluring. It just pains Leah to know how vulnerable Nicki is; more so now than ever before. She so doesn't want her to fall prey to the devil's schemes and deception. It's no small thing to be seduced by the most powerful and charming con artist since the beginning of time.

Oh, how she grieved to think, but she had to be honest with herself. Until Nicki comes to understand the difference between the two higher powers, the difference between God and Satan, there'd be no hope

DAVID ALAN SMITH

for her or anyone else for that matter. And to truly know the difference has proven to be extremely difficult; meaning chances are slim. '...*Narrow*...' is how Jesus put it. He says... '*only few*'...will figure it out.

Taking in a couple more terrifying videos as she chewed on Leah's remark that 'God is gone'; Nicki spoke up again. She wasn't satisfied with her mother's response; for two reasons. First, her mom was too lethargic. It bothered her to see that she wasn't on the edge of her seat like her. Secondly, she just flat out didn't care for Leah's answer. She couldn't bring herself to accept it.

"Come on, mom...! How could God be gone in all of this?" Nicki argued.

She was almost angry about it. But the angst was more about her shattered nerves than being contentious just to be contentious. There was really nothing about their surroundings to be mild and calm about. Besides, Nicki had every right to inquire about such matters.

"These storms, and earthquakes and, and—well all of this stuff, mom? You can't tell me this isn't God or..., or God doesn't have his hand in all this crap? What do mean..., he's gone...?" Nicki sharply interrogated.

It was enough to break Leah's gaze. She slowly turned her head to address Nicki, but before she could say anything, Nicki, doubled down. She fired

IT WAS A FREEWILL RAPTURE

out some more questions, but really — it was closer to Nicki scolding Leah.

"How could he be gone...?" Nicki charged. "Like..., what? Like gone..., meaning he doesn't see all this shit goin' down?"

Leah, this time engaged with a little more energy. "I think its Satan, Nicki — it's Satan that's doing all of these horrible things right now. I think God is just letting him do it."

"Ahhh geez — mom, can we just get off the Satan crap? I mean look at what's happening. This is God kind of stuff..., or maybe some..., some sort of alien attack thing. This isn't some little red fruitcake freak out of the Bible with a pitchfork and pointy tail." She barked.

Raving on, "You can't be telling me he's the one behind all this — this judgment or whatever's happening to us — that he's the one behind all of these kids vanishing and women no longer pregnant. I mean..., what the hell? What are you talking about?"

"NO...! NO...! NO...!" Leah stressed impatiently. "That was the Rapture, Nicki. Jesus took the Born Agains and the children, not Satan. Satan — well Satan's just capitalizing on God's miracle. He's using it to his advantage."

Being frustrated and short, "Oh, Nicki — never mind...!" Leah blurted as she threw her head down

DAVID ALAN SMITH

into her hands. She was mentally drained, and had a splitting headache to boot.

"It's too much right now Nicki. It's just too much to explain. Just know that it's not God. It's not God and it's not Jesus pulling the strings right now. God's not behind all these crazed demonic possessed people attacking and killing people. And it's not God that turned Sheefoo into a—well just know it's not God. That's all I can say right now."

Nicki, far from being even remotely convinced kept silent. Jeering and dismayed, she only became more defiant. As usual, her body language spoke volumes. She inconspicuously rolled her eyes and slightly shook her head in disbelief as she refocused her attention back on the TV with a scowl on her face.

It was, however, an opportune time for good ol' Dmitri to again jump in and feed the object of his deception; his special assignment. He's been inviting himself in every chance he'd get to gnaw on Nicki's brain like a pesky fly landing on food set on the table. With every crack she unknowingly opens up, in through the door the crafty demon will go. This is now the fourth time he's managed to do business with Nicki's mind.

He'll slither in and do what Influencers do best— convolute the truth; kind of like pouring paint thinner on a Rembrandt painting, smear it up and turn it into

IT WAS A FREEWILL RAPTURE

the equivalent of a preschooler's finger painting. God's indestructible truth is there; it'll always be there—for eternity. It's just, by the time Satan and his demons are through, it's so watered down and smeared in the minds of people that it's become unrecognizable.

"She's crazy...! And you know it. It's just stupid." He said very convincingly.

Nicki heard the thought loud and clear. So much so she again had to look over her shoulder to see who was speaking to her. Naturally, like she did before, she had to look at her mom to see if she heard it. But, no—Leah didn't hear anything of the sort.

At any rate, Nicki agreed with the voice she thinks she's imagined. The things her mom was saying, as far as she was concerned, did sound ridiculous; things that only an off-balanced lunatic would spew. 'Crazy and stupid'..., is right. She's heard many things about Satan; all kinds of things. Still, she just couldn't picture him doing all these incredible things across the globe. This isn't the devil's department, she figured.

So, what did she do? She went right back into trying to figure out God's role as the Higher Power in all of this malicious mayhem and carnage terrorizing all humanity. The things that are happening? This is god-like power, or highly advanced alien stuff from some other planet, she reasoned—not devilish pranks or things that go bump in the night.

∞ 189 ∞

Dmitri was, of course, right there to spoon feed her all the nutrients she needed to doubt everything her mother told her; just like Satan so masterfully did to Eve in the Garden. Satan had set the example as to how it is done. The devious blueprint has served them well for millennia. It seems like such a small thing; getting people to doubt. Yet, Dmitri knows the magnitude of its sting; the poison…, how deadly it is—like that of a black widow spider.

Going on Satan's lead, they know that doubt, any kind of doubt, even the slightest of doubt, is the one thing, and the…ONLY…thing needed to pry unsuspecting souls away from God's protection. It's all they need to get their foot in the door; and how easy it is to do. With just a few tiny words, they're able to captivate a mind and…, in turn—capture a soul.

Invoking doubt worked with Eve. Considering how many people doubt Adam and Eve's encounter with Satan is even true; one can only wonder as to whether or not their souls have been captured. Chances are…, they doubt it. Need one say any more about the beauty of doubt in the eyes of darkness? Or how it is that Dmitri knows all about the immense power and longevity that dwells within this itty-bitty thing called 'doubt'?

Leah went into the kitchen, mumbling to herself, probably praying as she often does is what Nicki

IT WAS A FREEWILL RAPTURE

assumed. Jeering, "She is crazy!" she told herself as she attempted to rationalize her mom's far-flung answer about Satan's role in all the madness.

Clearly, the tender loving compassion and heartfelt empathy she had for her mom immediately after the Rapture had dissipated. It wasn't entirely gone, it's more like it was put in check. It didn't take much. A handful of sophisticated words whispered into her thoughts would see to that.

Right now, she's entertaining the latest thoughts telling her that her mom is looney. It was the thought at the moment, yet it wasn't Nicki's mind that drummed up the thought. It was he, Dmitri—cozied right up against her ear, making himself right at home.

"She's not right in the head—she's lost it. But you've known that for quite some time now—haven't you." Dmitri insisted to make her feel smart.

Times like this, being so close to Nicki, close enough to breath in her ear made him relish the thought of being one of Vy-Gréthos demons, one of the Crossovers. To manifest in their dimension; to kiss, nibble, or even bite her ear to draw blood—so luscious and sweet, it'd be most pleasurable, he thought to himself. Still, he was quite content to know his place.

Besides, Influencers were far, far more superior than the Crossovers; in rank and abilities. They were a higher class of demons and recognized as such in the

∽ 191 ∽

angelic realm. Sticking to his domain, and happy for it, Dmitri persisted to sway his prey.

"She's off her rocker. I mean, how stupid is that—that it's the devil doing all these things. C'mon...! These are things that only Gods can do..., or aliens. With all these UFO's—maybe it is. But the devil...? That is insanely stupid—flat out stupid." He pounded.

Nicki just sat there and digested what she figured to be just thoughts. But..., 'things that only Gods can do'...? She could only wonder how that popped into her thinking. Weird...; was about all she could say about it. Gods...? Why 'Gods' as opposed to 'things that only God can do'. She pondered it for a moment, but it wasn't anything to dwell on; especially with the TV on—reporting on all that was happening.

A good hour would pass, and all the news footage, video feeds and reports were taking its toll on Nicki, Leah—everybody. There wasn't a soul alive that wasn't feeling the pain in one form or another. Whether it be empathy or experiencing painful accounts firsthand; the spirits of torment were clawing and gnawing on the hearts of people.

To see anguished mothers and fathers howl in tears; to hear them scream and breakdown as they'd testify and explain the loss of their children—it was hard to take in and process, let alone live it. From the wealthiest Kings, Queens, Senators and the biggest

IT WAS A FREEWILL RAPTURE

movie stars in Hollywood to rural school teachers, Islamic Jihadists and the Zimbabwe tribes of Africa; the horrific testimonies, tales and stories were the same in every language and every religion from every culture in every nation.

The mothers trying to describe how their babies were snatched out of their wombs; how they were unable to move as they watched the orbs move in and out of them leaving them empty and void of a due date. People broken and shaking as they'd confess to being forced to kill their pets and loved ones due to whatever it was that turned their beloved kindred into crazed, murderous and vicious monsters. On top of that; suicides continued to skyrocket.

Watching the death toll rise across the world with each passing second would leave everybody in question as to who was next or if they were next. It was all a guessing game. Billions were still separated from their families and loved ones. With one-on-one communications still shut down; not knowing where each other was at, wondering as to whether or not each other was safe, or dead or alive or taken in the Mass Vanishing would leave all of them swimming in the pools of unreserved fear and anxiety.

It was really getting to be too much. It was for Nicki. She was about ready to shut it all down and crawl under a blanket and pretend this dark nightmare couldn't possibly be happening.

Just then, standing there at the edge, peering down into the pit of hopelessness; ready to fall in—something happened. Just before midnight, a sign of hope stopped Nicki and pulled her back from the ledge. It was a beautiful sound.

"Ringggg…, Ringggg…," came out of nowhere. It was her phone. It was a beautiful sound, indeed; as Satan knew it would be.

Gloating, Lucifer speaking to Vy-Apheélion just before he'd give him the order to open the telecommunication spigot, "It'll be music to the ears of the desperate and tormented souls under our thumbs." He boasted.

Vy-Apheélion wholeheartedly agreed. And they were right. Finally, after nearly two days, to hear the phone's ringing once again was a glorious, unexpected surprise. It goes on to say it went far beyond being just well received. People jumped on the development like famished dogs; starving to death.

And Nicki Dawn was no exception.

1 Corinthians 15:51-52 *"Behold, I tell you a mystery: We shall not all sleep, but we shall all be changed — in a moment, in the twinkling of an eye, at the last trumpet. For the trumpet will sound, and the dead will be raised incorruptible, and we shall be changed."*

-Chapter Fifteen-
NO WHEELCHAIR

Charged with pure adrenaline, "Oh, my God!" Nicki shouted after her phone rang. She'd waste no time and answer it without even looking to see who was calling.

"Hello…! Hello…!" she frantically answered.

"Hello? Nicki…? Nicki…, it's me — Carla." A friend of Nicki's; one of the closer ones in her clique of about nine or so.

"Carla! Jeez, Carla — man! Am I glad to hear from you? Oh, my God! I haven't been able to get a hold of anyone since…, well — since all of this stuff started happening. Are you ok? Are you getting all this stuff? Can you believe all this s…t?" she clamored.

Nicki was so fired up and hysterical that she didn't realize how fast she was rambling, let alone how one-sided it quickly became with her barrage of personal questions. Carla, being just as wound up as Nicki, wasn't slow to answer.

Quick and sharp, "Yeah, yeah—I'm ok, Nicki. I'm ok, how 'bout you?"

"Arrrgh...," Nicki growled, "I'm goin' crazy, Carla. I just don't know. What the f... is happening?"

"God..., I don't know! I don't think anybody knows. "But..., you're ok, right? I mean—"

"Yeah, yeah, yeah..., I'm ok. I'm ok." Nicki assured, cutting her off.

They immediately went back and forth; flinging questions and answers at each other like a raving food fight. The intensity remained fully charged; neither of them lost any momentum. Eventually, the conversation swerved into what happened to Chad. Carla is the one who brought it up.

"Hey..., I heard about Chad. What the hell happened?" she grilled.

"Ah, jeez—Chad, I don't know. He like came over not long after that, that—whatever it was that happened. Were you held in place, Carla? Did you feel all that power or whatever it was?" Nicki asked without realizing she changed the subject.

"Yeah, yeah we all did—everybody did. Well...? I guess everybody except—I don't know? I guess there were some who were able to move during that freaky

IT WAS A FREEWILL RAPTURE

standstill thing, but they…, you know — they're gone. They disappeared…, or at least a bunch of 'em did — going into those glowing door things."

Nicki stayed silent for second as she pondered her mom's ordeal through the Mass Vanishing. She saw it firsthand. She thought about how her mom was able to move when it all went down.

"Christians — I think it was only Christians who were able to move." Nicki said almost somberly.

"Yeah, that's what I heard too. At least that's what all the reports and people keep saying. I heard a little while ago though, or now they're sayin' they think it was just the Jef Christians. Jeez…, who knows?" Carla grumbled.

"That's the adults though." Nicki charged. "But oh my God — the kids…, the children and babies, what's up with that? And did you hear they have yet to find a woman pregnant? They're saying that maybe there aren't any women pregnant which means no babies; no babies for what — another nine, ten months or more?"

"Maybe never…!" Carla quickly retorted. "Who knows what the hell is up? God…! This is insane! Frickin' crazy…!"

Nicki let out a heavy sigh at the thought. Carla, as if in perfect sync, did the same. It was brief, but the two had to absorb what easily seemed to be endless possibilities. Carla rekindled the conversation. Taking

DAVID ALAN SMITH

it down a notch, a little less excited she steered the conversation back to where they were before they got sidetracked.

"So! What about Chad, Nicki? What happened to him?"

"Oh man, Chad—well like I said he came over not long after the Mass Vanishing. We were all freaked out and stuff, and Sheefoo—she came out of my room, peeking out and scared." Nicki explained as she began to tear up.

She couldn't help it. She was hurt. Sheefoo was, in a sense, her baby.

Though distraught, she went on. "I…, well I picked her up and she was trembling, and I started to pet her and stuff, and bam! She—, she just attacked Chad like a…, a frickin' mountain lion. It was crazy—freaky. She just went to ripping into Chad like no one's business. Me and my mom, right away we tried to stop her, but wow—it was so fast and unexpected."

Nicki would break into a full-fledged cry as she reflected on Chad having to kill Sheefoo. "And then…, then Chad—he killed her. He broke her neck, but he had to—I guess. I don't know?" she cried. "I don't know if he had to. I think me and my mom could have caught her and…., and tossed her into the bathroom or something. But…, I don't know…, it was horrible Carla—just horrible."

∽ 198 ∽

IT WAS A FREEWILL RAPTURE

Nicki felt bad for Chad. There was no doubt about that. Hearing him scream for dear life was troubling. His wounds were nothing to minimize, but it was really Sheefoo, losing her precious little kitty causing her eyes to well up with tears. She took a second to regain her composure, and went on to wrap it up.

"After Sheefoo…, well after Chad killed her — we started to bandage him up and calm him down. We were all still freaked out; not only with Sheefoo attacking Chad but everything — everything going on."

"Yeah — we all are." Carla gently butted in. "And then what?" she added.

"Well. It wasn't long before his dad — I guess making the rounds trying to find him, came over here. He was worried about him being missing or not at home. Man, he was freaked out too. He was so relieved to find Chad though, but finding him all bloodied up and bandaged like some war casualty didn't help."

"Oh, man…, did you tell him what happened?"

"Yeah, we told him. We all told him what happened. He really didn't know what to say. He just walked Chad out the door into the car and who knows? Maybe he went home or to the hospital. I don't know. Now that the phones are working — hopefully they'll stay working — I'll try and get a hold of him to see how he's doing."

"Are you gonna stay home then?" Carla asked.

DAVID ALAN SMITH

"Oh…, hell yeah…! Are you crazy?" Nicki blurted. "I'm not goin' out there. Not right now—not with all those murdering freaks and animal attacks. I think its contagion. Until we know its halfway safe to go outside, I'm stayin' right here. We have some food and water, but still, I hope this isn't going to be a long wait. It's a scary thought. Anyhow, my mom and I are just kickin' it right now. We're just gonna stay here and keep watching the news to see what happens next."

Carla perked up, "Your mom, oh yeah—your mom?" She inquired. "I forgot. Isn't she, or wasn't she a Jef? Wasn't she like—like one of those Born-Again Christians or something?"

"Yeah…, she is." Nicki confirmed, almost embarrassed.

"So…, she isn't missing or didn't vanish?"

"No. She's here." Nicki said. "She's still here."

"Huh! Oh well—I guess it wasn't all the Jesus Freaks then—you know…, that vanished." Carla surmised.

Once again, a bit somber, "No, I guess not." Nicki agreed. She couldn't help but hone in on the thought of her mom again—how she lost her chance, how she could have vanished with the rest of her kind if she so decided. A sense of guilt would again creep into Nicki's conscience.

"Well—ok Nicki, I'll talk to you later. I'm gonna

IT WAS A FREEWILL RAPTURE

make some more calls. I still haven't got a hold of Lisa, or David — Chad either. Yvonne, Jase, Teri, and Philip, and..., and Bailey are all ok. But I guess Bailey and Philip were chased by some dogs though. She said about five of 'em; one of 'em was just a little frickin' chihuahua — the others though were bigger, and faster — she said. Pretty scary!"

"Dang...! Really — where...?" Nicki prodded. "Did they get attacked or..., or hurt?"

"Well..., no. She told me they were targeted for an attack, but they made it to safety — barely. Jumped over some people's wall into their back yard. Yeah..., and she said the people there were freaking out too — started yelling at 'em and chased them away — all pissed off. So..., they didn't get hurt or anything, but it scared the crap out 'em."

"Where...? Close by...?"

"Ahh..., I guess it was over by the Six Dollar Store — on Swan." Carla said.

"Wow..., not that far away." Nicki nervously mentioned. "Sheesh...! That's why I'm not setting one foot out this door until I know it's safe."

"Totally...! And, oh yeah...!" Carla added. "Yvonne's older sister, Genny — she lost her pregnancy and Teri's little brother, well..., I guess he vanished — it's what she said. She's ok, but she's pretty shaken up — her and her parents."

∞ 201 ∞

DAVID ALAN SMITH

"Man…, what's up?" Nicki mumbled in frustration.

"I don't know…, Nicki. It's…, it's all just crazy. From the looks of things, I mean they haven't really confirmed it, but some of the reports are saying it seems to be children no older than eleven that vanished. Some say twelve, even thirteen and fourteen, but who knows? I mean geez — where are they?" Carla demanded and continued to rant.

"Are they here…? Are they gone — are they dead? Like…, did they go to heaven? Are they just invisible or coming back? Were they frickin' abducted or…, or taken by aliens? I mean, what the hell — I don't know. Have you heard anything about any of this stuff?" Carla pried.

"Well…, yeah…, I guess." Nicki halfway answered; even though 'no' would be the answer to most of the questions Carla threw at her.

"I heard the reports too…," she said, "or at least some of them — that it was children twelve and younger. Thirteen, fourteen…? Like you said who knows at this point? It's still early. And like you, I don't know where they are or if they're coming back or if another round of taking more people is coming; I just don't know. I guess we'll just have to wait and see."

"What does your mom say, being a Jef and all?" Carla asked.

"Well…" Nicki murmured. "My mom says they're

❧ 202 ❧

IT WAS A FREEWILL RAPTURE

in heaven — taken by God, by Jesus."

"Jesus...? Oh brother," Carla scoffed, "I don't know about that."

"Yeah, well..., I don't either. But it was in the Bible that this was going to happen one day. My mom talked about it every now and then and it sure looks like it happened. You know, maybe they are up in heaven. I don't know. Maybe the Bible is true." Nicki reasoned, but with no enthusiasm whatsoever; almost hating to even suggest it.

"Humph...," Carla grunted and shrugged. "Really...?"

"Ahh..., Geez — I don't know Carla?" Nicki retorted with frustration. "Like I said..., we'll just have to wait and see what happens. Anyhow, I'm gonna make some calls too right now. I'll call Chad to see how he's doin'. Hopefully I'll get through. So, I guess I'll talk to you later, huh. And hey — let me know if you hear anything else, ok."

"Yeah, ok. I'll talk to you later, Nicki. I'm glad you're ok..., love you! And I'll tell the others, too — that you're ok, if you don't talk to them first."

"Ok..., love you too. Later."

After hanging up, Nicki was quick to share the news with her mom. Leah however was more interested in the fact that Nicki's phone was back up and running. Excited and eager, paying no attention to the

203

hour, Nicki called Chad's house straight away, even while she was telling her mom everything that Carla had told her.

Paying close attention, Leah waited to see if Nicki would get through. Sure enough, low and behold, Chad's mom answered after a couple of rings. From there it was the standard back-and-forth conversation in regards to everything going on, and in less than a minute, she was talking to Chad.

Watching and listening to Nicki talk on her phone perked Leah up. She too got somewhat excited. A spark of life re-entered her otherwise deadened soul. Like her daughter, over the last forty-some odd hours, she tried and tried again and again to get through to someone, anyone, even 911 on her own phone but failed miserably.

Joel was at the top of Leah's list. Speed-dial, voice-dial, manual-dial time after time, but getting through to him has been hopeless. She wondered about Joel. Actually, she wondered about everybody in her church; if she was the only one left. Joel however is the one she's known the longest; also, who played the biggest part in helping her turn her life over to Christ.

It wasn't but an hour ago that she was even reminiscing about how she and Julie were planning to meet up with him when he got back from Lake Tahoe—how Julie was going to surprise him by being there to greet

IT WAS A FREEWILL RAPTURE

him at the airport after all. She was so looking forward to talking to him and hearing all about his trip visiting his sister and brother. Now she just wanted to hear his voice, even his voicemail greeting.

She figured he was gone, taken in the Rapture. She wondered how it was for him; where he was at and what he was doing when all happened. In light of the thought of it though, she was finding herself somewhat torn. She was happy to think he was up with Jesus, but there was a part of her that wished he wasn't.

She knew it was wrong, that it was selfish, but she was so broken and hurt about missing her chance. She felt so alone, so forsaken and scared. Still, she was perked up. She didn't waste any time. It was now just past midnight but like Nicki, the hour really didn't matter. Not really knowing what to expect; she immediately speed-dialed Joel once again.

Praying...; praying to hear his voice, but not without first praying to hear the phone just ring. And it did—the phone started ringing. It made her shake even more with anxiety as she listened and waited for an answer.

"Hello...," came from the other end.

"Joel..., Joel...! Is that you?" Leah promptly asked.

"Uhh, no..., no I'm sorry this isn't Joel. This is Randy, my name's Randy. I'm Joel's older brother." Having seen the Caller ID on Joel's phone, Randy

❧ 205 ❧

DAVID ALAN SMITH

continued. "Is this Leah?" he asked.

"Yes…, yes, it is." she said having already begun to sob. "Is Joel there? Is…, is he there with you? Can I please talk to him?"

She so much wanted to hear Randy say — just a minute or he's out back — anything, anything at all to suggest Joel was still here. The hope was however short-lived. Randy wouldn't have such comforting words for Leah.

"Umm…, I'm sorry Leah, but — well Joel's gone. He's not here." Randy explained as gently as he could.

It was immediately quiet after that, but only for a moment. Randy easily detected the news he had for Leah was heart wrenching. He wasn't surprised to hear her break down. He'd hear muffled grunts, dead silence and a gasp for air, and again the same. He could tell she was crying uncontrollably. Leah doing all she could to keep her sorrowful cry silent didn't last long. Breaking and bursting into loud sobs and mumbling couldn't be helped.

Randy remained silent and politely let her weep. For a moment he thought about how and why she was here, still here on earth talking to him. Being that Joel mentioned everything about her, he knew that she, like Joel, was a Jesus Fundamentalist and shared the same beliefs. He wondered what the difference was between her still being here and Joel being whisked away.

IT WAS A FREEWILL RAPTURE

"Oh, uhh—I'm sorry." Leah shakily uttered after gaining some composure. "I'm..., I'm sorry, I didn't—"

"Whoa, whoa—don't be sorry, Leah." Randy interrupted. "I'm..., well—I'm just sorry I had to tell you the news. I know you guys were close. Joel had a lot to say about you—all good I might add; all good. He was extremely fond of you and thought highly of you. He used to tell me that you were the little sister he never had—that he felt closer to you than any of us."

Randy was quick to console Leah's grieving, but at the same time he was actually glad to be talking to her. It didn't hit him right away, but now that he had her on the phone, he instantly found himself wanting to ask her a ton of questions. He was longing for Joel just as much as Leah, but it was his knowledge of the Bible that he seemed to be starving for.

The Gospel, the prophecies, the Rapture, Old Testament, New Testament, Jesus; he couldn't help but suspect she knew everything that Joel knew and here she was—someone within earshot to take up where Joel left off. Once again, for a split second, he had to wonder why she was still here and Joel was gone. He was mystified. It was sure to be just one more question he'd have for her, but not now—later.

Right now, at the moment, never once losing sight of Leah's brokenness, he did well to sympathize with her. They were both grieving their loss of Joel.

∞ 207 ∞

DAVID ALAN SMITH

"Do you know what happened to him?" Leah asked with a sniffle.

"Yes. Yes, I do. I was there. I saw him go. Well—at least from the corner of my eye I saw him go. It was—I don't know. It was scary—scary for me, but Joel? Joel was—I'd say calm. He was calm, but excited at the same time. He wasn't scared. He looked like..., I don't know—like an over excited kid on Christmas morning I guess you'd say.

After that blast, that lightning bolt across the sky, and the darkness, and being held in place and all—God, that was weird. Shoot! I was freaking out. I mean—it wasn't only me, but all the cars, the traffic—it all just stopped. Ah, Gees! I'm sure you already know about all of that." Randy uttered after catching himself going off subject.

"Yeah..., Joel..., he was with me." he said with a little quiver in his voice. "He wasn't stuck at all, though. I mean..., we were both in the cab of my truck, heading to Reno—on our way to the airport and boom..., everything stopped. But it was the craziest thing—I couldn't move, but Joel..., he was..., he was able to move, no problem. And in seconds, wasn't more than 10..., maybe 15 seconds or so that he..., he just seemed to know exactly what was goin' on. Then..., he like..., leaned over and put his hand on mine—" Randy said and abruptly stopped.

IT WAS A FREEWILL RAPTURE

He choked up. He sighed and caught another breath. Clearly, he was still shaken up by the whole ordeal. Leah could hear it in his voice. She continued to listen with great interest as Randy moved to finish.

"I just couldn't move. I was clinching the steering wheel. I mean like really clinching it..., like white-knuckling it. I..., I couldn't let go. It was so weird. Anyhow, like I said he reached over and put his hand on mine to comfort me, I guess. He told me a few things—good-bye and stuff, and he just got out of the truck and walked over to whatever he saw and just like that—he was gone. He disappeared." Randy explained, still in disbelief.

"What do you mean—he got out of the truck and walked. He actually walked? The wheelchair," she excitedly pressed, "no wheelchair?"

"No! He didn't need his wheelchair. He was, I guess, healed or something. Joel actually got out and walked. I couldn't believe it, but then again, I couldn't believe anything that was going on at the time. Some lady—after everything that happened—some lady in another car said the same thing. She said she saw him get out of my truck and walk over to this—whatever the news is calling it— this vision, or doorway and he flat out disappeared."

He was ready to tell her more, but immediately stopped. It was because he again heard her choking

209

DAVID ALAN SMITH

up and weeping. Like the first time, he felt no need to rush it. He'd politely wait, and let her get it all out for the second time. Clearly, it was an emotional back-and-forth between the two.

After a few moments, still crying, "Changed — in the twinkling of an eye," she muttered softly to herself in between her sniffles and sobs.

Randy heard what she said, but he could tell by the tone of her voice that she wasn't really addressing him with the peculiar remark. He was curious though as to what she meant by it. Still, his curiosity wasn't enough for him to pry into it. He felt it awkward to do so; like it would be invading her privacy. So, he let it go.

Before he knew it, though, Leah followed up from her dreamy utterance. It wasn't but a handful of seconds that she eagerly delved a little further into what she saw as another prophecy come true; one that Randy had no idea or knew nothing about.

In tears, "He walked...? He actually walked...?" Leah pressed after catching her breath.

It would however be tears of joy that would escort the question. She was overjoyed to hear of such news. Randy immediately rolled with it.

"Yeah! He did. It was good. He actually walked." Randy happily shared as he switched modes.

He wasn't acting, so as to patronize Leah, he was truly happy to think about it as well. He told Jake and

IT WAS A FREEWILL RAPTURE

Rebecca the same thing, but they were nowhere near as ecstatic about the miracle as Leah was. They were too concerned about Sean and Skye's abduction, and losing Michael Ray to really appreciate the magnitude of Joel actually walking. But he understands where they're coming from too. By that, he doesn't at all question their lack of interest in Joel's departure.

Still, as far as Randy was concerned, especially at the moment, it was a cheerful thought and he couldn't help but jump right into Leah's moment to rejoice. There wasn't really too much out there to be happy about. So much misery, death, carnage, and fear; you name it—it was out there. So, joy of any kind or however slight it may be; it was welcomed wholeheartedly despite the darkness.

Just then, urgent and pressing, Nicki yelled out, "Mom! Mom come look at this. Quick! Check this out. Hurry…!"

"What is it, Nicki? I'm talking to Joel's brother right now. I need this."

Still clamoring, "Mom—just look at this. It's beautiful. This is good news."

Capturing Leah's curiosity, she moseyed over and peeked out her bedroom door to get a quick glimpse of the TV. What she saw was definitely eye-catching. It was enough to get her to take a couple more steps into the living room.

DAVID ALAN SMITH

"I guess there's an update or something." Leah said to Randy as she closed in, getting a better look at what Nicki was raving about.

Randy knew exactly what the hubbub was. Sitting in the back of the den, looking over Jake and Rebecca's shoulders as they perked up and scooted to the edge of their seat on the couch, he too was catching a glimpse of the miraculous event transpiring on the world stage. Rebecca and Jake were clearly as excited as Nicki was. Curiosity would also capture Randy's attention.

"Hey Leah—I really need to talk to you. May I call you up here in a while, maybe tomorrow morning—ten or so?"

Just as distracted, "Yes..., yes please do, Randy. I'd..., I'd like that. I need to talk to you as well," Leah agreed, almost in a rush.

She, like Randy, was eager to see what the ruckus was about. The phone call would end short and both Randy and Leah would sit down with their adjoining families and watch and absorb the newest update—a miracle. It was nothing short of fascinating.

Like the Rapture..., it too was bigger than life. Unbelievable.

Up next…,

THEY CALL HER THE
QUEEN OF HEAVEN

DAY OF THE LORD
DIARIES
~BOOK TWO~

— PREVIEW —

Dear Diary..., it's been hell on earth for the last two days. Certain Christians vanishing is one thing, but the children is another. Not only that, but the unborn babies were also raptured, leaving not a single woman pregnant on the face of the planet. The believers say Jesus took them, so as to spare them from the horrors to come; the Tribulation. Others are raising their fist in rage at whatever, or whoever abducted their children and babies. More later.

Dear Diary..., yesterday another miracle happened. They're calling her the Queen of Heaven. I can see why—she's so beautiful. She's a huge..., magnificent apparition that appeared in the sky off the coast of Portugal. She speaks only through mediums. She says she's the Holy Spirit of God—the Comforter..., the one Jesus said he would send, from the Bible. My mom says it's the devil—Satan. I don't know about that. All I can say is she's already proving to be heaven sent. She's doing things..., good things, great things that only God could do. She's bringing hope back into the world.

Still, I have to wonder.

...STAY TUNED...!

Contact Info: Email: *dayofthelorddiaries@gmail.com*

CPSIA information can be obtained
at www.ICGtesting.com
Printed in the USA
LVHW022028151121
703363LV00002B/110